T

Jordan Silver

Table of Contents

Chapter 1

CHASE

Stolen pussy has got to be the best fucking pussy in the world. Hands down.
"We can't keep doing this, you're marrying my sister remember?"
"Open your fucking legs, you know you want it Delia."
I forced her legs open. If she needs me to take the pussy to assuage her guilt then so be it, but I'm getting in there no matter what. Her bitch of a sister thinks she has me fooled, but I had news for her. No one pulled a fast one on Chase Thornton. I had a surprise in store for her ass.

I've been hitting the little sister for over two months now. I'd caught the sly looks and blushes that meant she was interested. I'd tried to ignore it in the beginning I'm not a complete dog after all. But in time I got to learn what her whore of a sister was up to.

I'm a mean, manipulative fuck. I knew if I ditched the bitch right away like I wanted to, I would lose access to the sweet pussy. Somehow I just knew the pussy was going to be good. So I set my seduction in motion. It wasn't too hard to draw the innocent girl into my web.
She was starved for attention and affection since her stupid ass family squandered it all on the bad seed.

Huh. Looks like she had them fooled too fucking twat. Celine hated Delia. She put her down every chance she got, personally I think it's jealousy. Anyone who had eyes could see that the younger girl had a more appealing allure. She was fucking gorgeous! At first I was just going to use her to hurt her sister, but then the game changed. At around the second time I fucked her.

She was just so sweet and unassuming, it was almost like she expected me to use her and discard her. I had a surprise for her ass too. She started to close her legs but I wasn't having that shit. Knowing what I was facing tomorrow, I was ravenous for her pussy, my pussy. I own that shit. I wrapped one hand around her throat while prying her legs open with the other.

"Open." I pressed down on her clit and she opened her legs, it worked every time. This girl wore guilt like a fucking talisman. I have to wear her down every time, but never in my life have I fucked anything so sweet, including her bitch of a sister.

I bit her neck as I pushed into her body. She bucked against me and made that noise she always makes when I first enter her body. It's a cross between a sigh and a moan and it gets to me every time. I wanted, no needed to mark her. All this time I'd been careful not to mark her where it could be seen. There was no way for the virginal lamb to explain away a hickey.

Tonight, on the eve of my grand finale, I let it all hang loose. I bit and licked and sucked on her neck as she clutched at me with her sweet pussy. She was at least a foot shorter, so my body dwarfed hers in the bed, which just turned me on more.

"Put your legs around me." She obeyed immediately, wrapping her legs around my ass. After I got her going it was always like this, easy sailing. She ignited under me and I could get her to do whatever the fuck I wanted, which was its own kind of high.

The fact that I was sneaking around in the middle of the night while the rest of her family slept down the hall was another. It had always been this way with us, the sneaking. Even when I would slip away from the office on her lunch break from classes and take her to a hotel. Sometimes she missed classes for the rest of the day. She'd gripe at me about that afterwards, but I didn't care. I wanted her pussy when I wanted it, no questions asked.

She never denied me anything. She gave me all the excuses and went through her usual spiel, which she needed to make her feel good about what we were doing. That's because she didn't know what I did, after tomorrow she will.

It was fun trying to keep the bed from making too much noise. She tried hard not to move but she couldn't help it. Every time I dug deeper into her pussy, her hips jumped. Her moans were getting loud, so I left off biting her neck to kiss her.

She almost bit my tongue the fuck off. My baby sure likes to kiss, fucking starved for love and affection; those stupid fucks. I'll show them though.

"Whose sweet pussy is this? I growled. "Yours..." She could barely get the word out so caught up in lust was she.

"You love me?" That was new. I knew what I was doing throwing that in there while her guard was down.
"Yes, yes, oh heavens yes." Her pussy locked down on me as she came all over my dick. I guess I got my answer.

"Fuck yeah baby come for daddy." I wanted so badly to let go and pound her pussy like I do when we're alone in a hotel. But I didn't want to ruin my surprise, so I held off. I worked her on my dick until she came one last time; I wasn't done by a long shot. I lifted up and off pulling her up with me.

I dropped back on my back, turned her around and fed her my dick while pulling her soaking wet pussy down to my mouth. She rubbed her pussy all over my mouth and face. My girl loved getting her pussy eaten out.

I could eat her for hours and she would be happy. She swallowed my dick the way I'd taught her. It had taken her a few tries to get it right I'm not a small man after all. John silver wishes he had my dick, just saying.

Anyway she's getting better at deep throating my shit, but I had to be careful she didn't bite down on my shit when I hit her G spot with my fingers, while nibbling on her clit.

When my little angel gets started she's hot as fuck and now was no different. With my tongue stuffed deep in her sweet young pussy, two fingers in her asshole, she was primed.

She hummed around my dick while I fiddled with her G spot, as her pussy flowed into my mouth like a never-ending stream. My face was covered in pussy juice and I loved it.

I'd stopped using condoms with her after the second time we'd fucked. I convinced her that it was okay to use the rhythm method; she was so innocent she bought it.

When she'd missed her last period, I'd convinced her that her body was adjusting to having sex for the first time. Why wouldn't she believe me? I'm a doctor after all.

After making her cum in my mouth I lifted her head off my dick, kept her head down in the bed, got to my knees and slammed into her from behind.

I knew she had trouble taking me from this angle; it was just a little too much for her small frame to handle. But as much practice as we've been having, she'd soon be over that.

I touched her cervix with the crown of my cock and pulled back. I didn't really want to hurt her after all, but I knew after a while she'd start getting into it and then she'd go wild. It never failed.

I bit her shoulder, her back, and her neck. Everywhere I could reach. I left my mark all over her as I fucked her hard, deep and rough.

She bit down on the sheet to keep her cries from escaping, as I grabbed both her hips in a tight grip. So tight! I was spreading her ass open as I pulled her back on my dick, which I was using like a battering ram inside her sweet, hot, tight as fuck pussy.

"Squeeze baby." She clenched my dick just as I'd taught her. She was already such a tight fit that the squeeze felt like a fist wrapped tight around my dick. She made me so fucking hot for her, with her little girl innocence in a siren's body, that I had a hard time keeping myself in check.

Her body shook as I pummeled her pussy. I'd gone so deep on that last thrust that I'd lifted her knees off the bed. "Unnhhnnunnhh...please Chase." She was pleading, moaning, as my dick bored into her.

"It's too much Chase please, please."
"No, the, fuck, it, isn't, take my dick like a woman." I purposely went at her cervix and she came off the bed. I was barley in time to catch her scream behind my hand.

She bit down on my palm and the pain went straight to my dick, which seemed to grow even more.
"You're in my tummy, I can feel you there, please Chase it's too deep." That wasn't quite accurate, but I knew what she was feeling. My girth was putting weight on her insides, adding pressure, it didn't matter she had to take it.

"I'm going to fuck you until you can't walk. How would you like that huh? I'm going to fuck you until the sun comes up. While your family is out there walking around and getting ready for the festivities, celebrating my marriage to your sister, I'm gonna be fucking you hard and deep. Right up against the door where they'll be walking back and forth." She fucking came and came after that. Hell yeah my baby is a freak.

***

I fucked her long into the night, finally letting her nod off around four in the morning. No one knew I wasn't on my side of the house, they had no idea I had been here defiling their youngest all night. I always gave her this room specifically, because it had a secret passage door that I could come and go from as I pleased.

It was easy to visit her from my bed, even with her sister here. I hadn't touched the bitch in almost three months. I gave her some cock and bull story about wanting to do things the traditional way, what bullshit. I'd already fucked the hair off her pussy, what fucking tradition?

As promised the next morning while her family was milling about outside, I had her up against the wall, her legs around my waist as I fucked her sweet pussy. Her mother had called to her at one point and I'd made her answer, even though she had been sitting on my face at the time.

Once, when Celine had come to the door to see what was keeping her, I'd had her legs around my neck. Only her shoulders touched the bed as I fucked her till she was damn near cross-eyed. I left her with a raw beaten up pussy, barely able to move. My pussy

I did remember to kiss her tenderly and cuddle her like the treasure she had grown to be. Even though she didn't quite understand that yet. I'd played my part so well you see, that no one, not even she who had grown so close, knew my intentions.

Chapter 2

CHASE

We were all headed for brunch. My brother Drew my sister Paulina and our parents. Then there was Celine and Delia and their parents Carl and Joann. Celine's family was from a middle class background, while we were what some liked to call filthy rich.

She'd caught me with her looks I have to admit. I'd been a real sucker for the hot blonde with the nice rack and girl next-door personality. What a con. It pisses me the fuck off when I remember how I'd even treated her like what she appeared to me to be, a lady. Dinner dates, long stemmed roses, weekend getaways. All the attention befitting the woman I'd decided to marry.

The first six months were idyllic. I really bought into her game. The mere thought had me clenching my hands into fists. I could beak her fucking neck, the conniving bitch. All in due time Chase, all in due time. I took deep breaths as they all exchanged bullshit greetings. The rehearsal dinner was tonight and tonight was the night all my plans would come to fruition.

"Uh, Delia, must you always look so...blah?" I looked up at Celine's admonishment before glancing over at Delia. It was pure jealousy talking there was nothing wrong with the way she looked at all.

Her peaches and cream complexion was healthy and glowing, no doubt from the fucking she had endured. That damn lady of the manor thing she had going on was heady as hell, at least to me it was. In fact, I thought she was looking fucking gorgeous for someone who was up all night getting the shit fucked out of her. And her lapis lazuli colored eyes had a fire in them that went straight to my dick.

I wanted to say something, especially when she hung her head, hiding behind her hair, blushing in embarrassment, but I didn't. I didn't want to tip my hand before the time.

"Really Delia, a turtleneck, could you be any more drab?" That came from Joann or Celine's puppet, as I liked to think of her. I looked to the father the sap to see if he would at least attempt to come to his youngest daughter's defense but nope. Nothing, not a peep, whipped dog motherfucker. I am going to enjoy what I have in store for this bunch.

My family said nothing but I could feel the disapproval coming off of them in waves. "Come sit with me Delia. I want to tell you about that new designer I found." Paulina to the rescue!

I know my little sister has a soft spot for my girl, though she could barely tolerate Celine, which made her mad as fuck. In fact, I was pretty sure my whole family felt the same way. That should've been a sure sign for me, but I was either asleep at the wheel the day we met, or the bitch was a first class actress. Knowing what I know now, I think it was a bit of both.

Delia made her way slowly around the table to Paulina's side head still down. I hated that shit. She was only supposed to be submissive to me, preferably when she was under me. I wanted to tell them all to go fuck themselves and leave her the fuck alone and then get her the fuck outta there.

"You're wasting your time Paulina, she wouldn't know fashion if it walked up and bit her." The smarmy bitch turned up her nose. I'd had enough.

"Celine..."
"What, why must you always defend her?" She was huffy. Careful Chase you don't want to give anything away, not yet.
"Because she's defenseless, now knock it off."

She was a little pissy because I brushed off her advances this morning after leaving Delia's bed. Not even if it was lined with gold bitch. I couldn't wait to get this piece of shit out of my life for good.

Chapter 3

CHASE

Brunch was a fucking trial. The fact that I didn't bitch slap Celine was a minor miracle. I tried to get the fuck away from her as fast as I could afterwards, but she cornered me.

"Chase, why does it seem like you've been avoiding me since we got here?" Did she always use to whine like this? Where the fuck have I been? Under a rock? What the fuck?

"I already told you why Celine, the wedding will be soon enough, just a couple more days." I gave her what I hoped was a reassuring smile but felt like I was hiding constipation to me.

"But it's been months already, couldn't we just, you know...?" She gave me her come hither smile, fucking anaconda bitch. I thought I was gonna be sick.

"No can do babes, plus I have to go see about things for tonight, all your friends are going to be there, don't want anything to go wrong."

I knew that would do the trick, the vain bitch was more interested in what her friends thought of the table decorations than she was in my dick.

What had I ever seen in this girl for real though? Was I fucking stupid or something? I mean she had a good act going, but when I took the time to look beneath the surface, it wasn't too hard to see what she was.

I got the fuck away from her and headed for the garage to collect one of my cars. I was feeling fast and furious, so I went with the Aventador.

I texted my girl on the way down the driveway, letting her know I needed to see her and where. My condo in the city would do nicely for what I had in mind.

I had no doubt that she would obey me. She didn't too much like the consequences when she didn't. A hard fucking was the least of her worries.

She got there twenty minutes after I did. "What took you so long?" I had my hand on her chin and not too gently either.
"Paulina..." I kissed her hard.

"I don't care who the fuck you're with or what the fuck you're doing, when I call you come got it? Now don't let that shit happen again."

I pushed her against the wall and caught her bottom lip between my teeth, then pushed the turtleneck up and off of her. Good, my love bites were coming along nicely; too bad she had to hide them for a while yet. I rubbed my engorged cock against her middle while undoing her jeans.

"What did I tell you about easy access? You know I hate these fucking things. From now on whenever you're around me it's skirts and dresses only. I don't care if they're long, short or in between; hear me?"

"Yes." There was no attitude whatsoever in that reply, she was already heated up. Good, I didn't feel like going through her guilty spiel right now.

"Hands against the wall."
She turned and did as ordered. I ran my tongue from the top of her ass to her nape, where I bit her again leaving my mark.
"Spread...wider…good girl."

I drove home without warning. Her cervix opened to accept me. I didn't need to be there anymore though since my seed had already taken root, so I pulled back.
"Cock that ass the way you know I like."

She arched her back deeper, sending me way deep inside her pussy. I grabbed on to both breasts, again not too gently, pulling and pinching on her nipples, which were hard as fuck as I plowed into her from behind, my teeth attached to her neck like a pit bull.

Slap...slap...slap, that 's all that could be heard as I pummeled her like a mad man. I was gonna make this up to her so I didn't let guilt at taking out my anger and frustration on her stop me, besides she loved it rough.

She was pushing back against me, taking my dick, her little hands folded against the wall. Her ass was driving me insane, so pert and firm and just fucking perfect. I smacked it and she creamed all over me.

"You like that huh." I brought my hand down on her other cheek hard, same results. Fuck, when was I going to get enough of her sweet pussy? Five hours before my rehearsal dinner and I was here in her pussy instead of with my wife to be.

I made her cum hard before emptying myself in her womb. "Tonight I want you to stay close to my family."
"But I have to stay close to Celine and her bridesmaids and stuff."

"Did she put you in her wedding party?" I already knew the answer to that, the jealous bitch. My baby girl hung her head in misery shaking it in the negative.
"Why not again? I can't remember the reason she gave me."

Yeah I did but I knew it was a bullshit lie. There's no way my little girl told her she didn't want to be in the wedding. And even if she had, Celine would never have taken no for an answer.

"All the other girls are blonde...."
Yet another reason to hate that stupid cunt. I pulled her into my arms and kissed her tenderly.

"You don't need to hang with them then, stick close to mom and dad and Drew and Paulina."
"But why...?" She looked confused.
"Don't question, just do. You drove your piece of shit truck here?"
"Uh huh."

That shit burned me the fuck up. Celine drove a brand new BMW that I'm sure they could barely afford, while Delia was stuck with a piece of junkyard heap that nobody else wanted. I think her old man got it off some old geyser friend of his. The thing was a fucking dinosaur. I remember Celine laughing about it at the time. We'll see who the fuck is laughing soon.

"Head back to the house I'll be there soon." I kissed my little girl gently to let her know we were good. Sometimes she needed lots of reassuring. After tonight, I'm hoping she outgrows that shit at least a little, and grow a backbone. In fact I'd see to it.

I had shit to do before I went back home. Shit that was gonna make a lot of people unhappy.
Like I give a fuck.

Chapter 4

CHASE

We're here this is it, or just about. I wasn't sure I'd have the stomach for going through the pretense of this fiasco; no one else was in on my little event. I could've told my brother, but in the beginning I didn't want anyone else knowing how stupid I was, then later the anger took over and I had to do it myself. It's mine to do, whatever came of it, I would take the backlash alone.

I searched the church for my girl to make sure she was where I told her to be. She was sitting between my mom and Paulina. Joann kept trying to get her attention, no doubt following Celine's orders to keep my baby away from my family. I had no idea what that was about, and quite frankly didn't care. Probably just more of her jealousy bullshit.

***

We went through the whole shebang according to the wedding planners' orchestration. Then it was time to head to the restaurant where we had a private room booked.

There were quite a few people there, extended family on my side, and friends on hers. I think only Delia and her patents were here from her family. Stuck up bitch was ashamed of her poor relations.

I checked once again to make sure that Delia was where I needed her to be before heading for the table with Celine her parents. Her best friend Maura and Maura's husband Dylan, along with some other people from the wedding party.

"Why is Delia over there? I told her to sit with us." She was pouting already. Shouldn't she be more interested in where I sat?

"What, I'm not enough for you?" I turned on the charm. You leave her just where she is bitch. "Of course you are sweetie, it's just she's so awkward. I don't want her making your family uncomfortable."

"She seems fine to me." I looked over to the table where my girl and Drew were laughing at something, probably one of his lame ass jokes. "Why do you always side with her?"

"Do I? I hadn't noticed."
Her jealousy was coming through loud and clear.

"Yes you do and I wish you wouldn't, she doesn't deserve such loyalty, especially not from my husband. I hope you're not planning to always be that way." Here comes the pout. It used to be cute but had stopped being that a long time ago. About the time I started hating her fucking guts.

We made it through dinner barely, with her prattling on in my ears about what changes she was going to make to my house and what invitations we would be accepting in the future, and some other drivel that I blocked out.

I didn't eat anything while I nursed my one snifter of cognac. I needed a clear head for what was coming.
Dinner was over and it was time for the toasts. I had asked my dad and mom to let me give the first toast before they did the whole welcome to the family bullshit. Not gonna happen.

"Hello everyone, I want to thank all of you for coming. If everyone would look this way." Celine and her mother were smiling, and my girl was looking like she wanted to disappear. I only had to put her through this one last thing and then she never had to worry again.

"As you know, Celine and I hadn't known each other very long before I popped the question. I thought I knew everything I needed to know at that point, so I bought the ring." There were murmurs and smiles at that.

"It was only a few weeks later that I got to really know her, and I must say it wasn't at all what I expected." As I gave the signal, a gentleman in the back cued up the movie screen sized monitor that I had brought in, especially for the occasion.

"May I see your ring?" She looked at me in confusion as she took it off, not knowing where the hell I was going with this. As the screen lit up voices could be heard.

"We're going to be living the life of Riley." On the screen Celine and Maura were reclining naked on a bed drinking what looked like champagne. They toasted each other while they giggled.

"So we're still on schedule right. Everything going as planned?"
"Yep. One year and then, it's freedom for the rest of my life. No stupid parents, and that annoying little bitch. I will miss his dick though, but the money to buy my freedom is more important."

"Oh I'm sure my Dylan can more than hold his own in the dick department, as you can attest to." They laughed and looked towards the camera, which they had no idea was there as Dylan entered the picture. You could hear a pin drop in the room.

"Turn it off." That was Maura, the maid of honor. I ignored her ass. The roomful of people watched Dylan and Maura fuck my fiancé in Technicolor. The lady like girl who lorded it over everyone else was into golden showers and drinking other people's piss. Her family and friends sat in stunned silence as I walked away towards my family's table. There was nothing more to be said.

I took Delia's hand. "Mom, dad, I'm sorry you had to see that but I had to do it this way. The fall out for our family is minimal if any at all. Forgive me for bringing this into your lives, I'm sorry."

"Forget about that son, are you okay?"
"Yeah mom I'm fine. I just need to get Delia out of here."
Her hand was trembling in mine and she was close to tears.

"Damn bro that's some cold ass shit." Drew was staring at the screen transfixed. Dad clapped me on the shoulder and asked what I was going to do now. Things were moving fast, people were getting up to leave, there were raised voices and recriminations heard in the background.

"I'm going to marry my woman." I swung Delia's hand up between us and kissed her fingers. My family somehow didn't seem as surprised as I would've expected, though it wouldn't have mattered. They hugged us both as I told them all, including her that we were on our way to Vegas in my private jet. By this time tomorrow, she would be my wife.

When we reached the doorway the screaming started.
"You bitch." She came running with claws drawn at Delia, but I got between them.
"Touch her and I'll not think twice about knocking you on your ass."

"So you've been fucking her this whole time and you have the nerve to judge me."
I had no desire to play out this soap opera any more than it already had, but I needed to answer that for Delia's sake.

"Actually no, I only started fucking her after I found out what a dog you are, and I have to say thank you. If I hadn't met you, I would never have found my treasure."

"She's not going anywhere with you, you're not going anywhere with him."
She made a grab for Delia's hand.
"I warned you."
"If you do this, then you're no sister of mine."

By this time Delia was in tears and I was over it. Her parents were still sitting at the table in shock, not even caring that I was about to make off with their daughter. Fine by me, we didn't need their permission or their blessings anyway.

"When were you ever her sister bitch? Why don't you go find a corner somewhere? Then again that's an insult to prostitutes everywhere. At least they're honest and upfront about what the fuck they are. When they fuck someone for money at least he knows the deal."

I was done with her ass; she wasn't worth it. "Come on baby let's get the hell out of here." She gave one last look to her parents and followed me out the room. Good choice.

Chapter 5

Vegas, was a hop skip and a jump away. We made it in no time and headed to the chapel I had reserved for the occasion. No cheesy shit for my wife, bad enough she was having to forego a formal wedding, but the least I could do is pick a decent venue.

I think Delia was in shock through the whole thing. It didn't matter, she answered when she needed to, and signed on the dotted line.

After that it was off to my island on my private jet where I planned to stay for at least a month. My dad was my partner at the practice. He'd already been planning to cover me for my honeymoon so there was no problem. There was still going to be a honeymoon, just the bride and the location had changed.

Celine had wanted to tour Europe. She wanted to see and be seen. My girl wouldn't give a shit about that.
"You okay baby?"

"Are we really married Chase, you really belong to me now?"
Fuck, how could two sisters be so completely different?

When I'd given Celine her ring she had spent the whole night admiring it. Delia on the other hand had hardly looked at hers, and I had made damn sure it was bigger and better than her sister's. Instead she was busy clinging to me like she thought I would disappear if she eased up on her hold. I really dodged a fucking bullet.

"Yes baby, I'm all yours." I had to kiss her she was so fucking cute.
"And we're gonna live together when we go home and everything?"
"What the fuck, babe that's what married people do."
"But what about my parents?"

"Your parents don't have shit to do with us. They can't do a damn thing, you're my responsibility now, not theirs, thank fuck."
"Celine is gonna be pissed."

"The fuck you care? She can't hurt you anymore babe, and don't tell me you'll be all torn up about having them out of your life because they were shit parents, and I don't even know what to call your so called sister."

"You don't know them Chase, they won't be happy that I took you away from their golden child."
"Fuck them, you're a Thornton now, those fucks won't dare fuck with you now, I'll end their asses. I don't want you worrying about this shit, you got better things to think about, like making sure my daughter is healthy and strong.

"Your daughter?" She looked surprised.
"Yes Delia, the daughter I planted in you two months ago."
"You..." She looked at me in shock before her hand went to her stomach in a protective gesture. She looked down as if expecting to see evidence of the child.

"But I don't feel any different."
"I imagine that will change soon enough. Give me your mouth." She complied, no hesitation this time. Of course I couldn't just kiss her and leave it at that I wanted my pussy.

"Turn around."

She's already sitting in my lap, so she just turned and straddled me, her short dress riding up.
I ran my hand from her knee to her pussy, and put two fingers in her heated cunt. She arched and moaned, thrusting her tits in my face.

"Open your top."
She popped open the buttons down the middle, leaving herself exposed. I used my free hand to open the front clasp of her bra.

"Feed me your tit."
She leaned forward, holding her breast out for my mouth. Now I was the one moaning.
"Take my cock out of my pants."

She wet my finger with her juices. Yes she liked me to order her around when we fucked which was just perfect, because that's just how I loved my sex. I was going to introduce her to some serious play on the island. So far we had only played around a little, I was about to go hardcore. Speaking of which.

I pulled my hand out of her pussy, licked it clean and reached across the seat to the jewelry box I had there. I took out the collar and clamped it on her neck locking it in place. Now she really belonged to me.

The collar had my family crest on a little locket that hit her throat. The lock in back could only be opened by the key I wore on a chain around my neck.

"Now everyone will know who you belong to."
That shit made me hot as fuck.
"Slide down on my cock baby." She did as she was told, taking me in nice and slow, until I was all the way inside her body.

I grabbed her ass with both hands while biting down on her nipple. She creamed my dick again; my girl is so fucking sensual.

"Please daddy."
"What do you want baby?"
"Faster."
"Wait."

She tried to rush me but one hard slap to her ass had her behaving herself.
"Ride my dick like I taught you." She placed both hands on my shoulders and rode me, up, down, back, forth, grind; repeat.

Five minutes of that and I was ready for a change.

"Pull off." She hopped off my dick and waited for direction. "Taste your juices baby." She dropped to her knees and licked my shit like a lollipop before swallowing it to her throat.

I let her do that for another five minutes before getting to my knees behind her and bending her over in front of the seat.

"Hold on."
She grabbed the arms of the seat and I fed her my dick inch by inch, until I was all the way home. Then I let her have it.

"What's my name Delia?"
"Daddy...oooh."
"Good girl, whose pussy is this?"
"Yours daddy, only yours."

Her pussy started to clench and spasm wildly. "Can you ever tell your daddy no if he wants to fuck?"
"No daddy, it's your pussy. Oooh, whenever...wherever, however, oh fuck me harder daddy."

I pounded the pussy just the way my freaky girl loved until I pulled out and came on her ass. I rubbed my cum in her asshole just for kicks and had her cumming again.

We fucked all over the fucking jet until we landed hours later. I had to carry her off the plane poor thing. She'd get use to my stamina in time no doubt seeing as how she was a good few years younger than I. I'm sure she could keep up.

The next month or so was to get her used to her new lifestyle. I planned on taking everything she had to offer. I also planned on spoiling her rotten. I planned on giving her everything her sister had oohed and aahed over, just to fuck with her, since I was sure we would be seeing her around. If she ever had the nerve to show her face in our small town again. Knowing that smarmy, narcissistic bitch she would.

I'm gonna make her regret ever fucking meeting me, but more than that, I was gonna make her regret treating Delia like shit her whole life.

Chapter 6

CHASE

It's day three on my island, it's been nonstop fucking since we got here. My girl seemed to be enjoying her newfound freedom. She was more relaxed, more carefree; in essence, more like the young girl she was supposed to be.

I've already started spoiling her her jewelry collection is off to a good start. I chose blue diamonds and blue topaz as a start because of the color of her amazing eyes. She's still a bit shy about receiving gifts, but I know that shit wouldn't last.

I plan on asking her about her fucked up relationship with her parents but not now, not here. I didn't want to bring that negativity here, but we have been talking.

She's more excited about the baby than I thought she would be. I thought I would have to talk her around. Do I feel guilty that I tricked her into it? Fuck no. It's what I wanted, so it's what I got.

I try to combat what I had seen with her family by being extra attentive and caring. But I realized that's not the way to go, I can only be me. She just has to learn that not all families are as fucked up as hers.

She knows she can say anything to me without retribution. She also knows she'll get her little ass spanked if she disobeyed me. I've been introducing her to fun play and toys for the past two days. So far she really likes the swing that's over the bed in the playroom, she loved swinging on and off my cock.

She laughed like a little girl on the playground the first time we used it, and has asked me to use it twice more since then. Of course I complied. Right now I'm introducing her to the stocks.

She's wearing five-inch spike heels that wrap high up on her ankles, black leather with silver buckles. They're hot as fuck. Her leather bustier doesn't cover her breasts, and her leather thong is a joke.

She can't see me obviously as I line up behind her. I heat an ice cube in my mouth, smoothing out the rough edges, before inserting it into her ass.
"Ahhhhhhh."
She wiggles her ass as the excess liquid drips down between her pussy lips.

I give her a love slap with the leather duster. I like to see her ass nice and red. Besides, she's on punishment, this morning my naughty girl wouldn't release my cock from her mouth when I told her to. She had to learn that I ruled. Everywhere.

I placed the stock bench between her ankles, spreading her nice and wide for my iron hard cock. But first there's something I want to try.

I lift her right leg in the chain until it's almost even with her elbow, not too high, I'm ever mindful of her delicate condition.

In this position her pussy is nice and open for me. I can see the different shades of pink that runs from her lips to inside her. I kneel behind her and drink from her cunt. Ambrosia.

"Oh, ooooooooh." She tries to fuck herself on my tongue but her movements are a bit hindered. I have her completely at my mercy.

I ease a vibrator in her ass; did I mention that she loves anal play? I've been widening her for future use. Her legs are shaking, the chain is pulling, but I don't stop. Eating her pussy is fast becoming my favorite pastime.

"Hmmmmmm, I love the taste of your pussy baby girl." I lick from clit to slit and back, all the while working the vibrator in and out of her ass on medium speed.

She's already cumming on my tongue; the shit is running down my chin. I work two fingers, then three in her, she's nice and soft and wet.

Her ass clenched against the toy as she squeezed my fingers, which meant it was time. From this angle I go straight up into her. With her breasts caught in my hands I ram into her from behind. I don't have to go easy because the stocks are padded around her neck.

I reached over and pulled her hair as hard as I could without causing too much pain, just enough to let her know that pain can be pleasurable.

I release her chained leg, working the kinks out before placing it on the floor. I never stopped stroking her though. Yes, tighter, my dick is happy. I feel the head of the vibrator rub against the head of my cock through the thin membrane; the sensation is unbelievable.

I pick up the clit teaser from the table next to me and put it against her clit. She clenched down on my dick like a vise as she tries to get away from me and fuck me at the same time.

"Keep your ass still." She stops all movement, on the outside that is, inside she's throbbing around my dick in a milking sensation. Yeah that's right she doesn't want to revisit the punishment chair and she damn sure don't want me to not let her cum, she says it hurts her tummy. That's one way to control her ass, because if there's one thing I've learned it's that she loves orgasms.
"Good little girl."

"Chase you're not moving, why aren't you moving?"

She sounded almost scared like she thought I was gonna leave her high and dry like I did earlier, but no. I needed this as much as she did.

My balls were full from watching her walk around all morning in her get up. It was hard for her to walk in her heels at first but she was getting the hang of it. I made her do housework in them get her used to them. I planned on having her wear heels all the time, three inches and up. Heels made her legs look fucking amazing, which made my dick hard as fuck.

She'd complained about that too which had added to her punishment. She didn't know it yet, but she will learn that she must never say no to me; my word was law.

I gave her a deep stroke to wet her appetite. I didn't want to cum too soon, she'd already cum I don't know how many times on my dick.

I loved the sounds her pussy made as I drove in and out of her. I pushed and pulled the vibrator in time with my strokes, in, out, in countering directions.

Her pussy was drooling, long drips of cum hanging to the ground. I was gonna enjoy cleaning her up after I off loaded deep inside her. "Cum for me baby."

The clit teaser, vibrator and my cock were too much for my little girl and she shook her way through one massive orgasm.

I wasn't too far behind as I spilled cum in the crack of her ass, I had other plans for her pussy. I dried the excess cum off my dick in her ass down to her clit, teasing her still throbbing pussy with the head. Her knees buckled and I hurried to release her.

I took her into the bedroom and laid her on the bed, she had her hand over her pussy. "What's wrong with your pussy?"
"It still tingles." I smirked at her; my girl was turning into a sex kitten.

I climbed between her legs on the bed and starting at her knees I licked up one and down the other, being sure to avoid her pussy. She mewled at me and tried to pull my head into her.

She got a hard slap for that one. "Stop."

When I was sure her legs were pussy juice free I concentrated on the main course. Eating her pussy until there was nothing left of her juices. She was a wrung out mess when I moved from between her legs almost an hour later but I wasn't done.

I pulled her to the end of the bed on her stomach while I stood over her and fed my hard dick to her. Her cheeks were nicely puffed as she held on to my hips and devoured me.

I tugged her head back and forth none too gently; it will be a while before I came again. "Use your teeth the way I taught you." She scraped them against the head and down again.

"Argggghhhhh, yes baby girl." Maybe I was wrong. Maybe it wouldn't take so long after all. "Look at me." She lifted her eyes to mine as I fucked her face, my dick in her throat.

She was hungry; she loved the taste of me as much as I loved the taste of her. "Get ready to swallow baby." I pulled back just enough to tap her tongue with my cock before going deep again. My balls drew up tight and I shot off in her mouth.

When she was finished swallowing I kissed her roughly before taking her into the bathroom to soak. "You did good baby." As usual I remembered to be tender with her afterwards. My baby needed all the love and attention she could get and I planned on seeing that she got it from now on.

Chapter 7

DELIA

We're going home today after a month on the island. I wish we could just stay here, but that's wishful thinking we both have lives to get back to.

Chase is on a mission. I understand that his pride was hurt, but it made me feel...strange. The one time I told him that his need to hurt Celine made me feel like I was just a tool, was the first time I had truly felt like he had any real feelings for me.

Don't get me wrong, I knew he liked my body and the things we did together, but even though he married me, and my little girl heart had wanted to believe it was true love, I never really knew for sure, until that day.

That day he had let me see a side of him that I think few people ever saw. It was raw emotion, so much. I will never again doubt his love for me.

It made it easier to face home again. If only I could talk him out of his need for revenge. Not only against Celine, but my parents, for what he deems their mistreatment of me.

He just didn't understand. My parents never wanted me, Celine was supposed to be it for them. I was a surprise, an unwanted one no less, and unfortunately they had no problem letting me know that from a very young age.

I'd adapted though, accepted my place in their lives for what it was, but they were the only family I had. I wasn't physically abused, but I learned that whenever Celine was anywhere around I became persona non grata.

As a small child it was hard to understand, but eventually you catch on and you step aside, stay in the background. You watch at Xmas when she gets a mountain of brightly wrapped gifts and you might be lucky enough to get maybe one or two, with a new book, or maybe if you're lucky a new pair of school shoes.

All their love had already gone to their golden child there was none left for me, but like I said, I adapted. Then Chase came along, and I think it was the first time since I was a very young child that I wanted something Celine had. I had long given up hope of ever gaining my parents' love, but this golden haired man, with a smile that made me melt, and the kindness he showed when we first met, it was like watering a plant left too long without moisture.

I blossomed under his attention, but there was no way he would notice me in that way, at least that's what I told myself.

I couldn't help the looks that I threw his way whenever we were in the same room together. Not that I had any intention on things going as far as they did. Who would pass up a blonde beauty for a mousy nobody like me? Which is the way my sister had always described me.

Chase made me feel beautiful, wanted, desired. It wasn't all sex toys and bondage either, that was just his playtime thing I called it. No, it was more than that, as I'd found out on the island when we were together, we were so happy.

I was gradually coming out of my shell. Though the gifts were nice, I didn't need them. Only his arms around me when we slept. The way he put his hand in the small of my back when we were walking somewhere, the way he looked right at me when we were talking, his laughter when I did something silly, his care for me and his unborn child.

***

Now we were headed home and I was scared, scared that there would be trouble, I know my family, especially my sister, and what Chase had done to her she would never forgive. The fact that he married me...hah, she will make my life a living hell.

"You're worrying again, I told you about that. You give your family way too much power; they're only that powerful in your head babygirl. To the rest of the world they're just a pathetic bunch who didn't have the good sense to recognize what a gem they had in their midst, their loss my gain.

Now stop worrying, everything's going to be fine. You're not Delia Fielding anymore, you're a Thornton now, and you know what my family name means in our town and yours. No one would dare mess with you, not even your family, you'll see."

"But Celine..."
"If she has the nerve to show her face she will be dealt with. If she causes you one moment of trouble I will bring her up on charges. There are laws against what she did after all."

"I just don't want any trouble."
"Come here, my little worry wart." I climbed into his lap, the safest place in the world. Unless he was laying over me in bed, that's when I felt my safest. Like he was a shield between me, and the rest of the world.

"You need daddy to take your mind off this stuff, hmm? You want me to occupy your mind until we get home?"
"Yes please." I was smiling before he got up with me in his arms and led us to the bedroom of his private plane.

Our clothes were gone. The sheets were soft beneath my back as he ate between my legs. One of my favorite things, he did it so well.

The sight of him there, this strong virile man who made me weak, when he was there feasting on me with his tongue it was as though I had the power.

My hands in his hair direct him, my sighs and moans and screams ordered. The way he feasted on my body said I owned him, just as he owned me.

I came on that thought, flooding his mouth with my juices just the way he liked.
"Suck."

Now it was my turn. I loved doing this with him; this too made me feel powerful. The sounds I could draw forth from him, the way his hands clenched in my hair. Oh I see this was to be more than just me sucking him, he was in an amorous mood.

He thrust in and out of my mouth forcefully, I liked it this way too.
"Take it all babygirl." My throat made room for his length; lots of practice had paid off. I could give him the pleasure he sought this way now.
"Look at me."

I look up into his eyes as I sucked him deep into my throat and out. I use my hands to hold him in place as I play with the very tip of him with my tongue.

He's long and hard and thick. This one thing brings me so much pleasure; I love it. I show it. I swallow it again as I play with the sac beneath, one of my hands goes between my legs; that drives him crazy I know.
"Fuck babygirl, enough."

I released him from my mouth, and he took the hand that I used to pleasure myself, sucking my fingers into his mouth as he drives into my body.

I cry out because he's so deep and it feels better than anything in the world.
"Shit, did I hurt you?" He clasps my face in his hands so he could look into my eyes.

"No, it was just all at once that's all." I was already moving under him, my toes clenching into the bed as he stroked in and out of me.
"I have to remember to be more careful with you."

I pull him down for a kiss and smile. He's already very careful with me, with us. Who would've thought my hard, angry man could be like this?

I lift my ass off the bed so I could draw more of his length into me. He's being careful now, I don't want careful. I want rough and hard and driven, like he can't get enough of what's between my legs. I bite him, that's my way of letting him know.

"Oh, someone wants to play."
My legs go up, up, he rears up onto his knees. My ankles are now held between his hands as he opens me wider. We both watch as he plunges into me. My wetness is evident all over his length the sounds make me crazy. I want more.

I look up at him and draw his attention. I bite my lip. I know what that does to him.
He drops my legs, attacks my mouth, plunging into me now at both ends. I try turning us over, he complies.

Now I'm riding him. I move faster and faster as the fever in my body heats up. My hips are a whirlwind, his hands and lips and teeth love my breasts. I'm leaking all over him; I can't stop.

I'm a dancer as I gyrate over him, but still it's not enough, he knows. He throws me off, climbs behind me and in one stroke buries himself deep.

"Yesssss, more, harder, deeper."

"Tell me what you want."
I'm still shy about saying those words.
"Tell me or I'll stop." He eases off, no, no.
"No, no, don't stop, please I need it, need you."
"Tell me." He gives a deep plunge, I grab onto the sheets with both hands as I push back against him.
"Fuck...fuck me...I want you to fuck me."

"Good little girl." And he gives me what I want. All of him, hard, deep, his all, now I'm happy. We ride out the madness together. The sting of his hand in my hair makes my eyes water but I don't care, this is what I love. This wildness that I can call forth from him, it makes me feel so alive.

Now for the tenderness. He's still hard as he pulls out of me, turns me over and reenters me this way.
Now it's softness, soft touches, whispers in my ear, whispers of love and devotion.
"Do you know how much you're loved little one?"
I shake my head; it's a game we play.
"All I have, all I am is yours, always. I'll never let anyone harm you again, never."
He kisses my brow as he releases his seed once more in me.

Chapter 8

DELIA

We've been back for a whole two weeks. I've returned to school and Chase to his practice. I'm finally learning to relax. I no longer expect to see one of them around every corner.

Chase, my husband, has gone out of his way to make me feel more secure. For the first week he drove me to and from classes, which took some maneuvering on his part because of work, but his dad was a big help.

In fact his whole family was helpful when it came to helping me get settled in. If Chase were too busy some other member of his family would be there for me. It was as though he sent out the memo saying that I wasn't to be left alone.

I was never left alone at any time except during classes. We still met for lunch, but now, because they were no longer stolen moments, we actually had lunch.

That's not to say that I haven't missed a class or two, and sneaking off to a hotel in the middle of the day was still fun. Unless Chase wanted to play, then we went to his condo in the city.

I'm now a little over three months along and he's being so sweet. Every morning when I wake up ready to die, he has dry toast and either tea, or a cold seven up waiting for me.

According to his mother it's the best remedy. Sometimes it works, sometimes not. Either way I always end up puking my guts up, which I would like to do alone, but he never lets me.

Sometimes I oversleep and awaken to find him dressed in one of his suits ready for work, just waiting for me to get up so he could help me through my ordeal.

He holds my hair, wipes my brow and supplies me with ice cold seven up. Sometimes my hormones get the better of me and I jump him for a change.

Thank heaven for afternoon lunches. Anyway, this is the end of our second week back and I'm finally relaxing. I haven't seen or heard from anyone in my family and I'm not quite sure how to feel. It's as though they've written me off completely, like I never existed.

Even after all they've done over the years it still stings. Chase's family is so supportive, so kind, they treat him like gold, and by extension me now too. It makes me feel small sometimes, since they knew what my family life was like, they'd seen it first hand.

Since we've been back I've learned that Sundays are the Thornton family day. No matter what was going on you had to be there for Sunday dinner at least, but they mostly spent the whole day together.

Paulina and I are pretty close since we're about the same age, and Drew's the big brother I never had. It's from Paulina that I learnt what happened after Chase and I left the dinner that night.

Apparently Celine had tried to save face by accusing me, and Chase of carrying on behind her back the whole time they were engaged. But the tale of the tape held out, no one pretty much wanted to hear anything she had to say.

Everyone had been disgusted by the three of them, and Chase had manipulated things so well, that the only ones in attendance that night were, her friends or people she wanted to impress. None of his patients or fellow doctors was there that night; thank heaven.

My parents had slithered away in shame, but I was sure all would be forgiven in time, they could never stay mad at her for long.

The Thorntons hadn't stayed around much longer after we left so I don't know what else happened after we left and I wasn't sure I wanted to know. That was a bad scene.

I have the taste for Rocky Road ice cream. I don't mean like 'oh, I could really go for some rocky road ice cream', I mean like 'if I don't get at least a pint of rocky road ice cream pronto I just might die.

Chase is going to be late getting home. I have the keys to my new Mercedes Wagon, there's nothing stopping me from running to the local market before it closes at eight.

I'm wearing lulu lemon yoga pants and a tank in black and yellow, because I just finished my stretches and because Chase says he can't resist my ass in them.

I grab my keys off the hook and head out, mouth already watering for that ice cream. I should probably stock up. The parking lot is all but deserted. Good, this means I can get in and get out in a hurry.

Of course no one in history has ever gone to the store to pick up one thing and left without buying out half the store. It's so good to finally be able to go to the store and buy whatever I wanted as opposed to what someone else liked.

When I'd let it slip that my mother's pantry was stocked with Celine's favorite foods he'd gotten so mad, he'd driven us to this very store and had me pick out whatever I wanted.

Let's just say I was a kid in a candy shop. No I didn't buy candy, well not just anyway. Since then he's been a bear about me getting things I like whenever we go anywhere together.

I had a cart full of crap, cereals and fruit, and snacks, and about five pints of ice cream. Time to cash out and head back home. Chase should be home any minute and I hadn't called to tell him where I was going. He'd freak for sure.

I heard a high-pitched screech and then felt pain in my lower back. I went down hard, and then...nothing.

***

CHASE

I was climbing into my car when my phone rang. It said babygirl on the screen. I smiled before I answered, probably needed me to pick her up one of her craving fixes. I should've called before I left the office.

She was the cutest little mommy to be, with her crazy cravings, peanut butter and strawberries for one. I tried to make sure we were fully stocked but she ate the peanut butter by the spoonful these days so we might've run out.

"Hi sweetheart."
"Sir, I don't know who you are, we found your number on speed dial in this lady's phone. You need to get to the Cloisters Grocery as soon as possible, the police and ambulance are on their way."

"Where's my wife, what happened to her?" To say my heart was going wild would be an understatement.
"There was some type of an accident here tonight sir. Your wife was knocked over in the store and she's been out for about five minutes."
My wife, my kid; my blood ran cold.

I was driving before I even realized it. I'd hung up on the lady on the phone without saying anything else. All I could think about was getting to her as fast as I could.

I got there in ten minutes. In that time a lot ran through my mind, not the least was what in the hell she was doing out this time of night by herself. Followed by what kind of condition I was gonna find her in when I got there.

I admit I was scared out of my fucking mind. If anything happened to either of them I don't know what I would do. She was my world my heartbeat. It still amazes me the way we met, how we came to be in each other's lives. That something so ugly could've brought about the most beautiful thing in my life, and I would be forever thankful for it.

I saw the flashing lights coming towards me as I reached the door of the store. There were about three or four people huddled over something on the ground.

I ran towards them and found Delia crumpled on the floor, an overturned cart lying scattered nearby. What the hell happened, had she tripped over her feet again?

I felt cold fear clutch my heart.
"Excuse me, this is my wife, someone called me..." I got down next to her and felt for broken bones, the whole time my heart beating out of control.

"That was me sir, I'm Justine Spooner."

"Could someone tell me what happened?" Was that me sounding so calm? I didn't feel calm.

"Yes sir, I saw the whole thing."
This came from an elderly lady who looked ready to do battle. By now the EMTs had entered along with the cops, wait a minute cops? Since when were cops called for a simple slip and fall?

"Let us through."
I told them who I was and that I was a doctor and divulged the information that Delia was pregnant.

I'd checked her over and there was no sign of bleeding but you never know. She would have to go to the hospital either way.

The same elderly lady who said her name was Myrna Jones was telling the officers what happened.
"And then she just hauled off and hit her, then pushed her and ran."

Wait a minute "What?"
"Sir let us handle it please."
Uh-huh sure. I kept my mouth shut and my ears opened.

I was already coming to my own conclusions but I needed to hear this to be one hundred percent sure. I felt my blood run from cold to hot, as anger like I've never felt pounded into me.

When she gave the description of the assailant I felt myself go into that place. It was a place that I steered away from as much as possible. It didn't do anyone any good when I went there, but every once in a while I visited it.
"Do you know who that is sir?"

What to tell them? Should I admit that I knew it was my sister in law and let them handle it? Or should I deal with this on my own?

Either way I would be the one to make her pay, but if I got them involved that might put a limit on how far I could go with my retaliation. On the other hand it wouldn't take much for them to look into our background, find the key players and put two and two together.

I had to think.
"Sir we're ready to transport your wife if you're coming with us."
"You guys will have to question me later I have to see to my wife."

I headed out the door reminding myself to find the old lady and thank her, and the one who had made the phone call, what was her name again? Oh yes Justine.

Delia awakened in the ambulance. I'd already called mom and dad to let them know what was going on. Of course they said they would meet us there.

"Chase?"
"I'm right here baby."
I held her hand and brushed her brow with my lips, my little girl. I felt tears prick my eyes. I don't think I would get the image of her on that floor out of my head if I lived to be a hundred.

I couldn't even bring myself to think about my daughter. I prayed that she was okay, that they both would be. Delia couldn't handle a loss like that it would destroy her.

"Do you remember what happened?"
"Somebody hit me, I think. I heard a noise and then everything hurt, then I fainted I guess."

She hadn't fainted she'd been knocked out cold. I felt the rage fighting for dominance, not now. She needs calm and steady right now.

But later, later I would take care of that bitch once and for all. I'd been almost tempted to leave it alone, for Delia's sake. To give up my need for vengeance, to maybe go only as far as seeing to it that Delia had the best things in life, but this meant war.

As soon as I was sure that my little family was safe, I was going on the warpath. That bitch fucked with the wrong one. I will destroy her, her mother, her father, any and everything she cherished on this earth would be taken. And if Delia or my child were harmed...well…let's just say there wasn't anything I wasn't willing to do.

Chapter 9

CHASE

Everything was okay thank heaven. Just a little bruising, a slight bump on the head, the little one was fine. Well, both my little ones were fine. I kept my anger in check. I didn't even tell her who had accosted her. I will of course, but later, right now I wanted us to concentrate on her and the baby.

I took her home, made her some soup and put her to bed. Poor baby, she was worn out with worry about the baby. I already knew I wasn't going to let this go, cops or no cops. They knew by now that it was Celine who had attacked her. They had her on tape, but wonder of wonders, she was in the wind.

No problem, I knew just how to smoke the bitch out. By the time I was through the Fieldings were gonna wish they'd never ever heard of me.

"Get some sleep baby, I'll be right here okay."

She was lying with her head on my chest. I wouldn't leave her until she was asleep she needed her daddy to make her feel safe.

There would be no sex tonight though her body had sustained enough trauma for one day. But I could still make her feel good in other ways. Hopefully I could stop myself from going too far.

I used long slow strokes up and down her back to soother her, while kissing her face. Her body gradually relaxed against mine. I palmed her stomach where my child was safe, letting my fingertips graze the top of her mound. She was very sensitive there, and it wasn't long before she was mewling and rubbing her legs against mine, fitting her little pussy over my cock.

Taking her mouth softly I held her head in place with one hand while I used the other to guide her hips in a grinding motion.

When her little hand cupped my rod and tried to release me from my pants I stopped her. "No baby, you need to rest, take it easy, I don't want to hurt you."

"But they said I was fine, and I feel okay. I need you, I need to feel safe." She was kissing all over my face, pleading with me to take her. Fuck, how can I deny her? I looked into her eyes as I laid her back against the pillows.

My shirt that she wore to bed was easily removed and I laid between her thighs so I could feast on her. I ate at her slowly, wanting to go slow, the taste of her pussy, so sweet on my tongue.

"Open."
She spread wider and I ravished her, making her scream and moan, begging me to take her.
"Not yet."

Her hands in my hair pulled but I stayed focused. I won't be rushed she needed tenderness right now. I will give her that if it killed me.

I kissed the place where our little angel slept, before kissing my way to her breasts. I made love to them while grinding myself into her; my pants were soaked with her pussy juices.

"Please."
She pulled my mouth up to hers and attacked my mouth with her own. I liked when she got like this, when she was the aggressor, my little tigress.

"Okay baby, I'm coming."

I only had enough time to lower my pants before her hand was there, guiding me into her warmth.

I closed my eyes in thanks, that they were okay, that we could share this. We moved together slowly, our mouths clinging to one another, her hands on my back urging me to go faster.

"No." I pulled my chest up so I could look into her eyes, my hands holding her head as I rocked in and out of her.
"Do you feel safe little one?"

"Uh huh." She ran her hands over my chest, as our movements became more forceful. Her legs locked around me, squeezing; looks like I won't be able to go slow after all. I switched us around, pulling her on top so she could ride. Her hands clasped my shoulders as I pushed up into her, while rubbing her clit with my thumb.

"Ohhhh, that feels so good." She rocked her hips back and forth as her body took over, her movements erratic, out of control.

I pulled her down so I could take her nipple between my teeth and bit down gently. She cried out as I turned her once more to her back. I kissed her eyes closed before kissing my way back to her lips. I emptied myself in her as she bathed me in her essence.

***

The next morning I made her stay in bed. Mom was coming over to watch over her, I had things to do, things that I refused to delay.

I pulled up to the Fielding residence unannounced. Joann answered the door with a weary look. Good.
"Celine's not here Chase, I wish you people would just leave us alone."
"May I come in?"

I didn't wait for her answer but pushed past her. It was the husband I was after, though she held much of the blame. I was raised to believe a man was the head of his house, whatever went on here, he allowed, whether by participation or neglect, he had no excuse.

"Carl, where's your daughter?"

"As my wife already told you, she's not here, we have no idea where she is." He looked like he wanted to disappear.

"You're lying, I know you are, you would never let your precious daughter go on the run without your help."
"Celine would never do what they're accusing her of..."

"They have her on tape Joann. Your daughter hit my pregnant wife and knocked her out cold. Now where is she?"
"Haven't you done enough to this family, haven't you destroyed us with your filth, what more do you want?"

"I destroyed you, I don't recall taking part in the filth as you so aptly put it. However that ship has sailed. I will warn you only once, tell me where she is or I will make you pay."

"How does Delia feel about your being here, does she know that you seek to destroy her family?"
"Family, what family? I'm her family my family is her family. You've never been a family to her, don't think you can start now."

"I don't know what that little tramp have been telling you but it's all lies, we were always good to her."
"Watch what you say about my wife...."
"She's our daughter..."

"Yes, the daughter you shunned and berated while putting that whore up on a pedestal. Listen, enough of this, just tell me where she is I don't have time for this shit."

She set her face mutinously and folded her arms. I looked to Carl but he looked everywhere but at me. Good, now I can carry out the decision I had made with a clear conscience.

"Don't say you weren't warned."
I walked out the same way I came in.
I had my phone to my ear before I turned the key in the ignition.
"Drew, remember what we talked about? It's a go."

I hung up the phone and headed back to the house. I think I will stay home today, dad will understand. Mom was already there when I got back. I wouldn't be needing her services after all. It was my job to look after Delia.

"Mom, I'm sorry I got you out here for nothing but I've decided to stay home today."

"That's alright son, Delia and I had a nice little talk. I think I'll go do some shopping for my grand baby, you need anything before I go?"

"No we're good."
I kissed her cheek and gave her a hug in thanks for being kind to one who needed it so badly. I will make sure that my girl was surrounded only by love. No one would ever be allowed to hurt her again, not if I could help it.

We said our goodbyes and I set Delia up on the couch in my study with her schoolbooks and her iPod. My decision to remain at home was two pronged. I needed to be close to her, after what happened I needed that reassurance that my little family was safe. And also, I knew that when the wheels that I set in motion started to turn, those vultures would seek her out. I will be a shield between her and them. They'll never get past me to get to her.

By one o'clock that afternoon my family's company that was run by my brother, had bought and called in the mortgage on the Fielding residence. Phase one of my open warfare had begun. Let's see how long it took them to play ball.

Chapter 10

CHASE

I know the shit's going to hit the fan as soon as their loan is called in, so I did everything to insulate Delia. They didn't have her new cell number, and my house phones were turned off for the duration. Anyone who needed me could reach me on my cell. So her parents couldn't reach her, and if they came to the office, that was fine by me.

I wanted them to come after me and leave my wife and kid the fuck out of it. I was sure that at some point they'll get to her, but that was going to be sometime in the distant future if I had anything to do with it.

She was out of school for the next week at least, that's as much bed rest as I could get away with forcing on her. She wasn't stupid. The doctor had told her that everything was fine so if I kept forcing the issue she'd know something was up.

I don't want her worrying about the destruction of her fucked up relatives. Celine was still in hiding but I had no doubt that with my resources I would be able to smoke her out before long.

I'm hoping her parents keep hiding her whereabouts though. I want them to play hardball so I can keep fucking with them, not that I needed anymore of an incentive. I just liked the idea of keeping them on edge, never knowing when the next shoe would drop.

I took Delia to our country estate this morning. We usually stayed at the condo in the city, it was closer to school and my office but it lacked the necessary security needed to keep her protected while I was at work.

Here she was well hidden behind an electronic gate that needed a code, not just to open but to call up to the house. So it wasn't like they could just randomly drive up and buzz the door. And if by some miracle they got past the gate, then she knows not to open the door to anyone unless it was a member of my family. I'm not taking any chances.

Last time I took shit for granted I almost lost them both. Not knowing where the fuck that psycho bitch was had me feeling extra cautious.

I checked her over before leaving the house. There was no bleeding, no tenderness, and the bruise on her head was starting to fade.

I set her up with her schoolbooks, DVDs, magazines, laptop, iPad, iPod, there wasn't a thing she could possibly need that wasn't on the bed with her. I didn't really want her moving around too much as yet.

My babygirl was alright though, both of them were, and that's all that mattered to me. I've been extra loving and tender with her. I knew when this shit was over she was going to have a hard time dealing with the fallout. Who the fuck could deal with assholes for parents?

Hopefully by then she'd have realized that she was better off without them.

***

I've been at the office for a couple hours already. Dad thought I should stay home with her one more day but I convinced him that she was okay there alone. I'd taken a ton of time off already and although my original plan was to take off longer, her injuries were such, that I felt comfortable leaving her on her own. Besides the bulk of my cases were scheduled for today. If I could knock them out then I could have a three-day weekend.

I've called home every hour on the hour though. I even found myself doing something I'd never done before, making a patient wait while I checked in with her.

She kept laughing at me because she would hang up the phone only to be answering it again in ten minutes as she puts it. Cute.

"Chase we're good, really. I haven't even moved, well hardly except to go to the bathroom. I'm going to get fat if I keep this up."

"You're perfect, just keep dong what you're doing. I know what the docs say but you took a pretty hard fall and you were out for a little bit. I don't want you overdoing it okay?"

"So you don't trust your colleagues?" She joked.
"No, when it comes to you and peanut I don't trust anyone but myself." The silly nickname for the baby was stuck, poor thing.

"Okay, can I at least make dinner for us tonight?"
"No, I'll be home in time to put something together, just concentrate on getting better. I put a sandwich and a salad in the little fridge. There's plenty juices and water in there as well, and those chocolate covered almonds you can't live without."

She squealed at that, such a girl. I sometimes forget how young my wife is. She still has a touch of the innocent left in her. It warmed my heart to know that in the short time we'd been married she'd started breaking out of her shell. She smiled more now, enjoyed things. Sometimes I would catch her playing with my choker around her neck with a dreamy smile on her face. I had explained to her that the choker meant she was mine in all ways forever. It seemed to give her comfort.

***

It's been two nights without making love. After she'd broken through my resistance the first night I'd put my foot down. That's a first since our wedding. I hope we didn't have too many more nights like those. This morning I was hard as fuck and my girl was needy, rubbing her heat against me, whining in her sleep. She missed her daddy's loving too.

Tonight though, tonight we'd be back to tearing up the sheets. I got off the phone with her after ascertaining that there had been no surprises, no one had tried to get in or call. Huh, so far so good.

It was four thirty in the afternoon. Charlotte the receptionist that I shared with dad had just informed me that my last appointment for the day was in half an hour and then I was free and clear.

It was a consultation with an elderly lady who already had an opinion from another specialist, but wanted a second opinion and maybe a third.

Dad and I had a reputation for no bullshitting. We took pride in our profession. Helping people or making them healthy if we could was our number one priority. Yes we made great money, but that's not why we got into the field.

My family has been well to do for generations so money wasn't an issue. Anyone who got into the medical field just to get rich was an outright asshole.

Anyway, because of mine, and dad's rep for straight shooting, and putting the patient's needs first, we had more patients than we could handle. It kept us both busy, which I never used to mind before. But now with Delia waiting at home for me in the evenings, I found myself resenting the time I spent away from her. She was fast becoming my everything, my whole world. That's saying a lot considering a few short months ago I had been ready to swear off women.

She wasn't like anyone else I knew though. She was genuinely sweet, naive and damn near innocent. In fact, outside of my corruption of her she was still relatively innocent. Funnily enough I wanted to keep her that way.

When the commotion came ten minutes before my last appointment of the day I can't say I was surprised. I'd expected it, been waiting for it almost, but I think I was still a little floored by their audacity.

I came out in the middle of Charlotte repeating her mantra of you can't go in there. Of course it was both of them, they travelled in pairs or packs like most vile things did.

"It's okay Char, I'll see the Fieldings. You can knock off for the rest of the day."
"Okay if you're sure Dr. Thornton, your father's still in his office if you need him." She gave my two visitors a suspicious look before grabbing her purse and heading out the door.

I led them out of the waiting room and into an empty office between mine, and dad's. I wouldn't dignify them with a visit to my private office they aren't welcomed, why should I pretend?

"Make this quick, I have a patient in a few minutes."
"We want you to undo it." Joann was her usual snarly annoying self, which meant I was ready to annihilate her ass coming out the gate.

"Undo what Joann?"
"You know what, you had your brother buy up our mortgage and call in the loan. Where are we supposed to come up with that kind of money?"

"I'm sure the bank gave you time to come up with it didn't they?"

"Ten days. Where will we get one point five million dollars in ten days?"

I shrugged my shoulders in a how the fuck should I know gesture. This bitch knew the deal; she knows what I want. I refuse to play her game. I don't trust this family at all. How they'd managed to raise my babygirl was a complete and total fucking mystery, because she was nothing like these monsters.

Not once had they asked about her. After hearing that their pregnant daughter had been attacked their only concern has been for her attacker. They could give a fuck about my wife and I could give a fuck about them.

"There's nothing I can or will do for you, if that's all, you need to go, I've wasted enough time on you already."
"We'll not stand for it." She moved to block my path, not exactly a smart move on her part.

"Stand for what exactly?" I folded my arms across my chest, spread my legs apart and waited. This ought to be good.

"We'll not be bullied by the Thorntons, just because you have money and we don't..."

"Stop right there. The "Thorntons" aren't attacking you, or bullying you. I am. Direct your anger towards me. I told you what would happen if you crossed me. Your fucking bitch of a daughter brought harm to my wife and child..." I shouted in her face, finally reaching my limit.

"Your wife and child, your wife and child, that's all you think about, what about Celine what she's been through? Do you think it's been easy for her? How can she keep her head up in our community after what you did?"

"After what I did huh. I don't recall being anywhere on that tape that was your bitch of a daughter and her greed. You really are a piece of work, now I see why she has such a false sense of entitlement it's all you. You're a joke; your tyranny of Delia is at an end. You want to keep Celine's whereabouts a secret, go right ahead, I'll find her eventually. In the meantime I'll destroy everything you hold dear, I will take everything from you."

"What have we ever done to you Thornton?"
"Oh ho, Carl Fielding, finally found your balls I see. I thought your bitch of a wife and whorish daughter had neutered you long ago. What was that again, what have you ever done to me? Nothing, absolutely nothing, other than spawning that bitch who humiliated me and my family."

"We had nothing to do...."
"Shut up Joann I'm not finished. You might not have done anything to me, but you did plenty to Delia, my wife, the mother of my child."

"You keep saying that but it's not true."
"It's not true? I didn't watch you for months belittling and putting her down, always choosing Celine over her even when she was wrong? I didn't hear the insults, see the put downs, did you think I was blind and deaf?" At least the dickless wonder had the decency to look ashamed. Too late asshole.

"That's enough Chase, you don't owe them any explanations. Mr. and Mrs. Fielding, I would appreciate it if you left now. The next time you come onto my property I will have you arrested."

"This is public property, it's a doctor's office for heaven's sake."
"You'd think so wouldn't you, but no, it's mine and I reserve the right to see whom I will. I don't choose to see you. Goodbye."

"You people don't understand..."
"I understand as a father that you two are severely lacking in the parental department. I understand that a member of your family sought to bring harm to my son."

"Delia's a part of this family too..."
"No, she's a part of mine. I haven't seen any part of you in her. She's a sweet, kindhearted young lady who now falls under my care as head of this family. Trust me, you don't want to piss me off anymore than you already have. Stay away from my son and my new daughter."

"Just as I thought, bullying tactics." Dad laughed her off. I kept quiet and let him finish them off. I had no idea he felt so strongly about the whole situation, but the anger was coming off of him in waves. We'd discussed the issue of course, but not once had he let on that he was this angry.

I should've known. Both my parents loved my Delia and were looking forward to their first grandchild. I had no doubt dad could use his formidable power to bring them down, but I don't want him to. This is my fight I have to do it, for her.

Maybe some of that was my guilt for how I'd treated her in the beginning, when I'd set out to use her for my own end. But mostly it was because I hated what they'd tried to do to her. Dad's voice intruded on my thoughts once again.

"Call it what you will, I'm sure my son has already told you, but if he hasn't let me warn you now. Delia is now a Thornton, she carries the name and is accorded everything that comes with that. That means she now has access to heads of state, not only in this country, but quite a few in other parts of the free world. She's not to be touched, if she so much as stubs her toe while you're in the vicinity, run and hide...Chase you have a patient waiting."

Dad turned and left. I raised my brow at the now sheet white pair. Oh well. I had only intended to play with them for a while, but papa bear had brought the hammer down on them. I wanted to laugh my ass off.

"If you'll excuse me, unless you have something to tell me?" I waited to see if they would give her up. Carl made as if to speak, but once again, was beaten to it by his lovely wife.

"We don't know anything, this is just an attempt to get back at us for some imagined slight against that...that...She spluttered as I felt my ire rise. If she wanted to play it that way, so be it.

"I warned you against speaking against my wife, but as usual you choose to ignore that. As my father has said, you've overstayed your welcome, leave or be escorted from the premises."

I watched them walk out the door before leaving the room myself. "That's one nasty piece of work there son, he's a complete tool and her, well, I think she's a bit deranged. You and Delia, be careful."

"We will dad, not to worry."
"Okay son, you go see your patient, I think I'll hang around 'til you're done for the night." He looked at the door where they'd disappeared.

I hid my smile. See that's a father, still watching out for me although I'm a grown man, I will never stop being his responsibility. I'm glad Delia had that now too. My sister and her were always chatting away on the phone, or it was her and mom. Even Drew and her were building a fondness for each other, though their relationship was a bit more antagonistic.

Drew being the overgrown ape he was compared to her tiny stature loved to make fun of her. She gave as good as she got though, and now instead of cowering, or trying to blend into the woodwork, she had laughter and teasing.

All in all things were good except for her family's continued existence. After my consult I called Jameson for an update on his search for Celine and was disappointed once again to learn that there was o sign of her. Disappointed but not completely put off. I know it's only a matter of time. In the meantime...

Joann had finagled her way into the pretentious country club set that she erroneously thought was a way into my mothers' good graces. Though mom did attend certain charity events there, my family hasn't been members for years. Not for lack of trying on the committees' part though.

I know the yearly fees are astronomical. Another sign of how they stretched themselves beyond their means to appear to be something they aren't.

I'm sure they'd been relying on my marriage to Celine to afford them certain things in the long run. I wonder if they'd listened closely to that tape, if they'd heard her talk about shedding them like unwanted refuge. Probably not, they were so blinded by her that they probably just heard what they wanted to.

I called up Janice the head of the committee who was only too happy to comply with my wishes. Seems she was none too fond of Celine. Yet another person she had pissed off with her snotty bullshit attitude, and Joann of course was thrown into the mix.

***

Delia was taking a nap when I finally made it home. I watched her sleep for a little while without disturbing her. She looked at peace, her soft peaches and cream skin smooth and glowing. Her tummy was barely noticeable but I could see evidence of my child in her growing breasts.

Looking at her made my chest tight, my heart hurt, my knees almost buckled. Life was so fucking strange. Who would've thought that I would find this, out of all that ugliness? How did I ever get so fucking lucky to find such a treasure? It didn't seem real at times like this, when my mind was clear of everything else, and it was just, her, and I. When I took the time to really think of us. It seems so far fetched that this amazing person was in my life. I'm not sure I deserved her but what the fuck, I'm keeping her.

I snuck downstairs quietly to make her favorite spaghetti Bolognese and garlic bread with Caesar salad. Cooking relaxes me, so I felt more of the day's tension leave me as I puttered around the kitchen. When everything was ready and warming in the warming dish I went back upstairs and climbed into bed behind her.

Folding her back against me, my hand covering the slight mound of her stomach where our child rested, I kissed her temple softly. "Wake up sleeping beauty."

She scrunched up her cute little nose, eyes fluttering open before she turned over in my arms with a sleepy smile. "Hi." She placed her hand on my cheek." I missed you."

"I missed you more, dinner's ready." Why was it that whispering in bed, no matter what you were talking about seemed more intimate? She threw her leg over my hip, rubbing her pussy against my rapidly swelling cock. My gym shorts offered very little protection against her heated core.

"Love me first, please. I miss you."

I pulled her bottom lip down with my teeth before licking inside of it with my tongue. Cupping her ass cheek in one hand I pulled her over on top of me fully, so her clit fit right over the head of my already leaking cock.

She didn't need any direction as she ground her pelvis against mine. "Hmm, put it in, I can't wait, please it's been too long."

Pushing my shorts down to my knees I released my fully erect cock. Pulling her thong to the side I pushed her down until I slipped into her.

My pre cum and her natural lubrication made it easy to slide up into her. Placing both hands on my chest, she pushed back and down until she had all of me buried deep. Sitting up she pulled her tank top off and threw it to the floor.

"Ride me babygirl."
Hands back on my chest, she pulled up and sat back down on my dick before rotating her hips in circles, rubbing her clit against my pelvic bone.

Taking her hips in both hands I pushed up, digging deep, searching for that little patch of rough flesh inside her with my dick head. When I found it she groaned and clutched me tighter.

"Give me your nipple baby."

She pulled up until only my cock head stayed inside the opening of her pussy and put her tit in my mouth. I bit and sucked it deep into my mouth as I slipped the tip of my middle finger into her tight, hot ass as I sat up, driving my dick back in to the hilt.

She came with a purr, body trembling, legs quivering as I continued to pound up into her soaking wet snatch. Fucking into her while she came had me on the brink.

The pressure against my cock was almost too much as I pounded against her cervix. Every once in a while my crown peeked into her womb before I pulled back. It wasn't enough in this position. I'd been without her for two days and apparently that was too much.

I released her nipple, lifted her off my cock and positioned her on her hands and knees in the middle of the bed. I started eating her from behind, paying special attention to her reddened engorged clit, before sticking my stiffened tongue into her, then pulling out and licking back and forth to her rosebud. Getting to my knees behind her I led my dick into her tunnel with an almost punishing thrust.

"Fuck, fuck, fuck, so tight, so good." I could go deeper from this position. I watched as I slid in and out of her heat. Nice slow strokes that teased her. She pushed back at me. "Chase, please."

I watched her ass clench and quiver as she drew me in and tightened around me to keep me there. Hunching her ass, she rode my dick from tip to base.

"You missed me, did you miss this huh?" I kept teasing her, not giving her the pounding she liked when I took her doggie style. "Yes, yes, oh yes, please, please, please."

"Please what little girl?"
"More, more, more, make me cum, please Chase I need to cum."
"Play with your clit baby...yeah, that's good, now taste yourself."

I pounded hard as she put her fingers in her mouth and sucked as she came. Pulling out I went around to her mouth and fed her my cock. She licked me from crown to base before taking me into the back of her throat, humming around me the way I liked.

Her beautiful face was a study in ecstasy as she concentrated on giving me head. I played with her hollowed cheeks as she licked my pee shoot. Pulling her mouth away, I kissed her rough and deep. Two fingers found their way into her over heated pussy as she came in my hand.

She went back for my cock when I ended the kiss, more ravenous now. Fuck I didn't want to cum in her mouth, not this time.

"Ease off baby..."
I had to practically force my dick out of her mouth. Pushing her to her back I climbed between her legs and pushed into her. I had her legs over my back, and her ass wriggling on my fingers as I teased her rosebud.

I pounded into her like a madman, trying to make up it seemed, for the two days we'd lost. Her pussy had a stranglehold on me as I thrust in and out of her. She looked up into my eyes and the look of pure love I saw there was my undoing. I felt tingling in my legs, down my spine, as my balls tightened, and my dick strained for release.

"I'm cumming, shit, fuck...Arrrrgrrrhhhhhh."

"Cum in me, I want to feel you cumming in me, fill me with your cum." She dug her nails into my ass just as I shot off. My orgasm triggered her own as she impaled herself deeper on my dick and screamed. I emptied my balls into her, clutching her tiny frame close as we came down.

As I slipped out of her, not completely depleted, my overflow followed my dick out of her pussy. I used my thumbs to open her up. I loved the sight of my cum, thick and creamy at her opening. Using two fingers I scooped some out and fed it to her, watching her swallow before licking her lips.

"Uhmm, yum, goody." She stretched like a cat and I smacked her ass before pulling her out of bed.
"Shower imp."

"Uh-uh, I want to eat like this, with your cum running down my legs. I want to be able to feel you as I move around." She was talking like a sex kitten and blushing bright red, it made me grin.

"You want to drive me crazy you mean, cock tease." I swatted her fine ass.
She poked her tongue out at me before taking the shirt I'd worn to work and pulling it on, leaving it unbuttoned. Of course, what better way to tease her poor husband while he ate dinner?

I shrugged and pulled on my robe, our juices drying on my dick, as I followed her down the stairs to the kitchen. We ate sitting at the island, every other mouthful followed by a French kiss or a finger fuck in between bites. We kept teasing each other all through the meal and I was enjoying this new playful side to my wife.

She was coming more and more out of her shell, her sexual appetites matching mine. She was such a joy to behold as she teased me. Laughing at her antics, watching her finally so carefree and uninhibited, helped to reaffirm my vow to keep her safe always.

If this game that I started with her parents continued for too much longer I might have to make some changes. Maybe I'd have to up the game. Instead of just destroying them socially and financially, I now wanted them out of town completely. I didn't want them and their poison anywhere near her again.

Getting them thrown out of the country club, taking their home, these were just the beginning. I will turn them into social pariahs; my campaign had only just begun. Even if they were to come to their senses and give up Celine's whereabouts, I would still continue on my path. I hated them with everything that was in me, hated them enough for both of us.

She brought me back to the present with her foot in my lap rubbing my dick. I pulled her into my lap and sat her on it.
"Mouth." I kissed her as I pushed my shirt off her shoulders. Picking her up I laid her on the island and gave her what she wanted.

"I love you babygirl" I was cuddling her in my lap after another mind-blowing orgasm. She smiled at me, that little girl smile she always wore whenever I praised her for something, or like now, when I professed my love for her.
"I love you too daddy." My heart melted.

Chapter 11

CHASE

It wasn't easy keeping her distracted for a whole week, so the following Monday I grudgingly sent her off to school. We'd spent the weekend out on the water. We didn't go out too far at first because I wasn't sure if her tummy could handle it but she was fine.

We spent the whole day being lazy on the boat. I taught her how to man the boat, to much laughter and fooling around. I'd found a little inlet where we anchored and I took her on the sand after a picnic lunch.

Now my stomach was in knots as I buckled her into the jeep. "Call me if anything happens today okay. I don't care what it is if you feel frightened at anytime I want you to call." She cupped my cheeks in her hands.

"What's wrong, why are you so afraid?"

I kissed her brow. I still hadn't told her that her sister was the one to hurt her. I just told her to stay away from her family and I said it in such a way that she knew I meant business.

I wish I could stick someone on her to follow her into the classroom. I didn't feel comfortable letting her out of my sight and out the gates.

"Nothing's wrong, I just don't want you hurt." I looked into her eyes, so precious. My hand was drawn to my child in her womb, both my precious girls.

"I love you okay."
"I love you too Chase." She grinned at me cheekily. "Now let me go or I'll be late." She gave me one last smooch before I stood from my crouch and closed her door.

All day I was on pins and needles, waiting for the phone to ring with some disaster or other. I know Janice had given the Fieldings their walking papers. I didn't know how she did it, wasn't interested in the details. All I wanted was for them to be thrown out with no chance of a refund. Petty I know but so much fun

They'd starved my wife of affection her whole life. Giving her hand me downs which in itself is not a bad thing, but they spoiled Celine, giving her the best of everything, while Delia looked on. I'll never be able to get that picture out of my head. The things I imagined she felt when she was made to watch on Xmas and birthdays when Celine got anything she wanted, while she got next to nothing.

Just thinking about it spurred me into action. Before I knew it I was heading out the office on my lunch break. My first stop was the Jeweler's. I got her a new charm bracelet with a teddy bear and a peanut for the baby.

Next up was a furrier's, where I found her the plushest white blonde fur they had. She'd be set for the winter months.

I found her a couple designer bags and a few evening clutches. Not that I knew what the hell I was doing, but the sales lady was a big help. She chose this brown and tan canvas bag with an LV logo all over it that she swore was all the rage for young women in Delia's age group. Plus one that she said although more matronly was a very high luxury statement.

I took two of those, one in black and one in their signature orange. I had no idea these things actually cost so much; women are crazy.

I headed back to the office loaded down with my loot. There had been no phone calls and it was coming onto time for Delia to be returning home. As soon as that happened I would be able to breathe easy.

I went through the rest of my day giving my patients the care they deserved. I could do no less, but I kept my ear out for anything.

I made it through the day with no surprises and headed home at a decent hour, to find my beautiful wife making dinner.

She is the messiest cook in creation. I lived by the clean as you go method, Delia liked to get flour and whatever else she was working with all over the place. Pots and pans in the sink, the skin from whatever peeled vegetable on the butcher's block.

In her bare stocking feet she barely reached my chin as I walked up to her and hugged her from behind. She gave a little start at first because she hadn't seen me come in, then she relaxed against me with a sigh.

"Hi honey."
"Hi baby." I bent and twisted my head taking her lips in a slow deep welcome home kiss. She rubbed her ass against my already hardening cock, bringing it to full life.

"What are you making baby girl?"
"Stroganoff."
"You want it to burn?"
"Nuh uh."

"Then stop rubbing against me like that or I'll take you upstairs and fuck you." She shivered and pressed back harder.
"Do me."

I pulled on the collar that she always wore, with my teeth, as I pressed my cock harder into her sweats covered ass.
"Take them off." I helped her shed her pants as I released my belt.

"Undress me." She turned and knelt in front of me, biting her lip as she pulled my zipper down. Without having to be told, she took my dick out of my silk boxers, licked her lips, then my cock head.

I fondled her chin, lifting her head so I could see her eyes as she pleasured me. Her tongue made swirls around my tip before she swallowed me. Sucking back and forth as she fondled my balls, rolling them against each other.

"Enough..." I pulled her up and lifted her light- weight high bringing her pussy to my mouth, while her legs went around my neck. We probably made a sight. Me, with my dick shooting straight forward, hard and dripping, my pants around me ankles stopped there by my shoes, her short frame held up by my hands on her ass as I ate her pussy.

Her sharp claws in my scalp alerted me to her oncoming orgasm. "Cum in my mouth." I bit her clit and she filled my mouth with her essence.

Laying her back across the island I surged into her, our eyes locked, hands clasped as we bonded. I covered my daughter with one hand as I took her nipple with the other.

"Always so beautiful Delia, my Delia." She clenched and came, so easy to please, so beautiful in her release. She pulled me by the tie I was still wearing and I went in for the kiss we both so desperately needed.

"Uhmmmm...squeeze me baby...just like that…again." I pulled her up and off the island and stumbled walked to the living room, my dick still inside her. With every step she squeezed tighter.

I laid her down on the fireplace rug and fucked her. Long, hard, deep thrusts that had her body sliding across the floor.
"I...can't...get...enough, never enough, fuck me, so sweet, so fucking sweet."

She babbled some shit back at me but I couldn't hear as I had gone dumb, deaf, and blind. The orgasm slammed into me like a freight train and took over all my senses.

When I was done shaking and groaning I found that I had pulled her legs over my shoulders and had doubled her almost in half.

"Shit, did I hurt you?" She shook her head and blushed while she giggled.
"No, it was fun, I liked it. You don't get so wild anymore. I was beginning to think the passion had worn off."

"Is that what you think? That my darling girl will never happen." I punctuated each word with kisses.

"Now that you are well and truly fucked feed me, but first lets go clean up. I hope I didn't spoil dinner baby...."
"No, it's perfect it should be just about ready."

The next day I wasn't as nervous about sending her off, but I had resigned myself to the fact that I was always going to feel that slight pang every time we parted. I guess it was part of being in love. Plus it was nice to see her hitting her stride, getting her confidence back.

She'd squealed with delight when I gave her-her presents, going on and on about Louis somebody and Hermes. Hell if I knew, but as long as she was happy, I was happy. She had me clasp her bracelet on her wrist and announced that it was never coming off.

That's what I love about my babygirl. I'd given her diamonds and emeralds among other things fit for a queen, but she found more delight in a much less expensive charm bracelet, because it represented our child.

I went to work smiling and happy. My step was lighter; things were coming along just fine. If all goes well I would soon know the whereabouts of my enemy and I could close the book on that chapter in our lives.

I should've known better than to let my guard down.
I was in the middle of a consultation when I got the call. When I saw 'My baby' calling, my heart almost stopped. I knew she had a class at this hour. I knew her whole schedule down to the second.

"Excuse me I have to take this."
"Go right ahead Dr. Thornton." I excused myself and walked over to the window.
"Baby, what's wrong?" Fuck me she was crying too hard to talk.

"Mom, mom, my mother..."
"Where are you?" I didn't mean to bark but that's just what it sounded like.
"School, come."
"Is she there right now?"
"Ran away...hiding..."

"Stay on the phone I'm coming."
I ran out the office with my heart in my throat.
"Dad I need you, I gotta go..."
"Is it Delia, the baby?"
"I don't know, her mother is at the university I gotta go. I have Mrs. Singleton in my office for a consult can you cover?"
"Go ahead son, call me as soon as you can."
"Will do." I yelled back over my shoulder as I ran out the building.

I didn't force Delia to talk, just listened to her breathing and talked to her calmly, telling her I was coming to get her.

"I'm on my way babygirl. I'll be there soon, how's peanut, she okay?"
"Ye...yes, nothing hurts, she just, she scared me, she was so angry and I thought...I thought...."

"You thought what baby?"
"I thought she was going to hit me." Her small, little frightened voice was the last fucking straw. Fuck this shit.

I had her give me directions to where she was hiding out in the outer room of the Dean's office and ran in to get her. I didn't see any sign of Joann, lucky for that bitch.

Kneeling in front of a frightened Delia I folded her into my arms and stood. I thanked the elderly lady behind the desk and told her I'd be taking it from there since she seemed genuinely concerned for my girl.

"When you're ready to make a complaint let me know." She handed me a business card with her name on it and I left. I walked out making sure there was no danger around. I'd forgotten how snakes reacted when cornered. I knew it was a bad idea to let her come back here now, but I also thought they'd heed my warnings, apparently not. Well we'll see about that.

I buckled her into my car and drove away. She was curled into a ball. How many times had I seen her like this after they'd fucked with her? This wasn't supposed to be happening, her marriage to me was supposed to put an end to their tyranny. They wanted to play hardball okay; it's on.

I took her home, gave her a bath, and made her some tea, before asking her any questions. "Okay, from the beginning."

" I went to lunch with some of the other girls. When I got back she was just there on campus. I didn't even know she knew what classes I had and where to find me." She was starting to hyperventilate.

"Deep breaths baby, come on."

She calmed down enough to tell me that after she had dismissed the other girls, telling them that it was her mother, Joann had ripped into her. Accusing her of having them thrown out of the country club and trying to run them out of town.

"Why does she think I did those thongs Chase, how could she?" I had to tell her the truth. "Because I did it." Her mouth fell open. "I told you what I was going to do."

"I know but..."
"There's no but, it's done, and now after this little stunt things are just gonna get worse for her, them. Don't even think about pleading their case with me, you'll never win."

Then I dropped the hammer on her and watched the life almost die out of her eyes.
"My sister..."
I nodded my head and barely made it out of the way as she ran for the bathroom where she was violently ill.

I followed behind her and helped her up when she was done, then back to bed. I held her as she cried her heart out asking over and over again why they hated her so much. That was something I needed to know myself. Time to get some answers.

I waited until I was sure she was asleep before slipping out the house. I drove straight to the Fielding residence with murder on my mind.

As soon as they opened the door I barged in and went for her. Woman or not, she'd crossed the fucking line.
"You crazy bitch, didn't you hear me the first time?"

I'm not ashamed to say I had her by her fucking neck as she scratched and pulled, calling to her husband for help. He came over to us but I was too fucking pissed to give a shit.

"Wait your turn asshole, you're next. What the fuck were you doing going after my wife?"
"What?"
"I said stay the fuck out of it Carl, I'll deal with you later."

"Joann what did you do?"
Fuck, these people never listen, oh well.
"I went to tell her the truth about her precious husband."
She spat out the words like venom.

"You thought I was pretty fucking precious when I was about to marry your slut of a daughter."

"Celine deserved something good in her life, after all your wife destroyed it."

Her words were slightly garbled but I heard her loud and clear. "How the fuck did Delia do that? She didn't birth herself you sick fucks. You were her parents, you're her mother..."

"No I'm not, I didn't spawn that, that, thing." I dropped my hand like I'd touched hot coals. "What did you just say?" I took a step back, what game was she playing now?" She smirked at me, evil bitch.

"Your wife is the product of a dirty old man's lust. An old man who took advantage of an impressionable young girl, my daughter."

What the fuck?
"What are you saying?"
"Delia is Celine's daughter."
"That can't be, she would've had to be..."

"Thirteen that's right. Your precious Delia is the product of statutory rape." There was a gasp from over my shoulder and I knew who would be there before I turned around. I caught my wife before she hit the floor.

"Who?" I turned back to them as I clutched her to my chest. Joann folded her arms and her lips but for once Carl Fielding had a pair. He spoke up before she could stop him. "Vito Escalante."

"Carl..."
"Enough Joann, it's out now no use hiding it from him." She didn't look too pleased by his little revelation but that was the least of my worries.

Chapter 12

I took her straight to my parents' mansion after calling dad and begging him to come home as soon as possible. There was no way they were going to convince me that Vito Escalante was a monster. I knew the Escalantes, they were nice people, and more than that he was my fucking godfather.

The only reason he hadn't been at my wedding was because he had to be out of town. A business deal that they'd had in the works before we'd set the date. His wedding gift had been a cool two million dollars. I've known this man my whole fucking life. No...fucking...way.

I had bigger problems on my hands though. How the fuck was she going to take the fact that I slept with her fucking mother? What a fucking mess. I wanted to be sick but I couldn't think about me right now. I had a pregnant wife who had lost consciousness twice in as many weeks. The stress from this shit wasn't going to be easy, and now this. I wanted to rail at something, to slam my fist into something. How many more knocks was she expected to take?

Mom was there when I got to their place. Delia had barely come around, and was groaning like she was fucking dying. I'd yell at her later for sneaking out and following me. She could've put herself in danger, as it stood she'd taken a hard shock to her system and before the day was out she would face more.

How did I feel about the fact that I'd slept with one woman and married her daughter? Not good, but fuck it, it's not like I'd set out to do it. I refuse to be held accountable for something I had no control over. Delia's the one that worried me. She was already so wounded, what was this going to do to her?

How was I gonna fix this cluster fuck? I had to tell my family. I didn't expect them to feel any differently about it than I did, but it had to be put out there. This was my doing not theirs. There was no shame, not for me anyway, but Delia I know would be a different story.

"Bring her inside Chase. I've got your old room all set up." I carried her up the stairs and asked mom to leave us. Before I talked to anyone, I had to settle this with her. I didn't want her dwelling on this shit and hurting herself fuck that. They'd taken enough from her already; I'd bear the brunt of whatever came from this. But not her, she was the only innocent in this whole fucked up fiasco.

Laying her on the bed, I pulled the covers up over her, it seems like I've been doing this a lot lately. "Talk to me baby." She was barely aware that I was there it seems, having shut herself down. That couldn't be allowed. It wasn't good for her, and it wasn't good for the baby.

"Delia, I said talk." I used my forceful tone, the one I used while dominating her, or when I wanted her to know I meant business.

"I don't understand, help me understand please..." I took a deep breath before I began. I had to tread carefully here. This shit was a minefield, and though I didn't believe that Vito had raped anyone, something had obviously happened. Why else would they use his name?

"Okay, from what your…Joann said, it seems that Celine had you when she was very young...I'm not sure about all the details as yet but I promise you that I'll find out...."

"If she is my mom, then I..." She covered her mouth with her hands and fled the bed. Fuck...shit...I followed her and brought her back when she was done. She held her body stiff and I knew this was it; this was the moment that will either make us or break us.

"I slept with you and you were going to marry my mother, what does that make me?"
"You, didn't do anything, I did...we didn't know. How can we be held responsible for what we didn't know?"

"I can't, I can't, I can't...."

"What can't you do?" There was no point in getting angry she had a legitimate reason for feeling the way she did. It's fucked, but it's true; but I'd be double fucked if we were gonna lose each other over this. No way I was letting them fucking win. She's mine, she's gonna stay mine.

"I did a bad thing."
"Okay Delia, listen to me now, the fact that Celine might be your mom, does that change the way she treated you your whole life?"

"But I ruined hers...."
"Would you treat peanut this way, for any reason?" She quickly covered her stomach with both hands. "Of course not, I would never...no."

"So there was no excuse for the way they treated you, get that through your head okay. Now there's something else you need to know."

How the fuck did I do this?
"The man they're accusing of being your father...is my godfather." She started again, body flinching, face losing color.

"Listen to me Delia, as soon as I'm done here I'm gonna call him, and we're gong to get to the bottom of this. He's not that type of man. He'd never molest an underage child, so either Celine lied about who fathered her child, or something else is going on here entirely."

'Do I have to see him?"
"You don't have to see anyone if you don't want to. All you need to do is rest and take care of yourself and peanut. You haven't done anything wrong, I promise you this. There's nothing for you to be ashamed or scared about."

I brushed her hair away from her face. At least she didn't flinch away from me that time. "Do you believe me?" She nodded her head as her eyes began to close.

"Do you still love me?" I held my breath waiting for her answer. She pulled my head towards her and kissed my lips. It wasn't a blazing passionate kiss but it was enough for now.

"Look at me Delia. I will take care of this; we will be fine, nobody's going anywhere. I don't care if Celine is your mother or sister it makes no difference to us. The only one who should feel guilty about any of this, is me. I'm the one who went after you, you understand? You have nothing to feel guilty about, please don't beat yourself up about that." I said it but I knew she would, that's why I had to get all the answers.

It was sheer providence that I got a call from Jameson telling me that he'd finally found Celine. "I'll send the plane to get you, bring her in." I didn't wonder about how he was gonna pull that off. I don't care, if he had to hogtie the bitch so be it.

I went and found mom and dad, filling them in on what the hell was going on.
"Vito would never do such a despicable thing."

"I know dad, that's why we need him here. I need to look in his eyes when I speak to him...."
"Call him, you know your Godfather will come for you, just call."

I reached for the phone and made the call. The Escalantes lived only about twenty minutes from here. The three brothers, Vito, Santino, and Rocco were recluses. They had more money than Croesus, but for some reason never married, never had children and still lived together in their rambling old mansion.

"He's on his way. Mom I'm going to need help with Delia, if this turns out to be somehow true, then I'm afraid of what it'll do to her mind...I...I slept with her mother…." I couldn't even finish. It was one thing to tell yourself you didn't care, that there was no doubt, but saying it out loud like this, especially to my parents, made it seem too fucking real.

"Son, the fault is not in you, you had no idea. Now granted you shouldn't have been messing around with Delia while engaged to Celine, but you explained the circumstances and why you acted the way you did. You weren't having relations with both at the same time; that would've been harder for her to overcome. This might take time, but I believe Delia's a strong girl, she'll bounce back."

"I hope so because I'm not letting her go...ever."

"It'll be fine son, remember who you're dealing with here. These people are pure evil you saw that first hand, we all did. No matter what, there's no excuse for the way they treated her, whether she was their daughter or granddaughter. Do you think your mom and I could've ever treated you or your siblings this way, for any reason?"

What he said made sense. I knew these things, but I was so worried about her fragile state of mind, all the stress of the last few months, now this.

"Look who I found." Drew came into the study followed by Vito. My godfather was about dad's age maybe a little older, which would make him late fifties early sixties. He had a full head of hair, walked with a cane because of some boyhood injury, and still had a sparkle in his eyes.

I looked at him for any resemblance to the girl upstairs. I couldn't find any. Then again, I was suddenly so tense it was a wonder I was still standing.

"Maxwell, Rhina, you look lovely as usual." He greeted my parents before coming to me.

"My son, what is it I can do for you? You young people are always in a hurry, what is it that couldn't wait until I finished my round of Warcraft? I had Santino beat this time for sure."

I almost laughed at that. I wondered how the brothers survived living together for so long since they were all so competitive with each other. Then again that's how they'd grown their family fortune over the years.

"I need to ask you a very serious question." He studied me when he realized the seriousness of my stance. Before I could say a word Delia walked into the room. Vito turned, got one look at her and went sheet white.

"Tessa, how...where...?"
He turned to look at the rest of us.
"Who's Tessa?"

"My sister, but it can't be. She died forty years ago, right before I met you, remember Maxwell?"
Dad said he'd forgotten that when he met Vito at university he had mentioned losing a sister the year before.
He walked over to Delia but I got in his way.

"What's going on here, who's this girl?" He tried looking around me.
"My wife, now come sit here, I need to ask you something."

I led him to a chair since he looked like he was about to keel over. He couldn't take his eyes off of Delia.
"So it's true then...." I couldn't wrap my mind around that. Vito had raped an underage girl?

"What's true?"
I cleared my throat. How did you ask a man you'd respected and loved your whole life if he'd raped a young girl?
"Did you ever know a Celine Fielding?"
"Fielding, Fielding, why does that name sound familiar? I never met a Celine, but the name sounds familiar, maybe someone I did business with?"

"No, this is the girl who says you raped her when she was thirteen and got her pregnant."
"Wh...what, are you insane?"
"Vito, just hear him out, he's not accusing you of anything we just need answers. This is a very delicate situation we're dealing with here."

Dad calmed the situation while mom held Delia on the couch, rocking her back and forth. I wanted to go to her, to comfort, to shield, but she needed answers now, we both did.

"Boy you know me better than that. I could never do such a thing."
"I didn't think so, so I need you to think back eighteen nineteen years ago. If you had any strange encounters with a strange woman or girl?"

"Well...back then I was a...ahem...a bit of a playboy if you will, so that would be hard to say. But I know for sure none of them were underage. I usually found my game around here in bars."

We went back and forth for what seemed like hours getting nowhere. One thing was for sure. If Delia bore such a striking resemblance to his sister then she was somehow related to him. Could it be one of the brothers had used his name? That didn't make sense either, why would they? They were each wealthy in their own right, all good-looking men.

"And you say this...is my daughter?"
"We think so."
"But how, why?"
Just then my phone went off.
"Jameson...come on up."

"I think we're about to get some answers, but keep in mind these people lie."

Jameson came into the room with a struggling Celine under his arm. "Put me down, how dare you." She screeched before he set her on her feet.

"You, I should've known, why am I here?" She spat venom at me with her eyes after removing the blindfold she'd been wearing. "You remember Vito don't you Celine?"
"Who?" She looked at him in confusion. There was also something a bit off about her, she looked...high.

"Did you drug her?" I turned to Jameson before he could leave.
"No sir, that's how I found her. Lets just say she was in a uh...compromising position trying to get a fix." I dismissed him after that.

"You don't remember Vito, how about you Vito, does she look familiar?" He squinted at her studying every angle in her face.
"There's something about the eyes, but no, I can't say I've ever met this young lady before."

"What's this about Chase, who's this man and why did you bring me here?"
"It's about your daughter...."

"My what? What daughter?"
"Delia...."

She howled with laughter, bent over, belly aching laughter. "What the hell are you talking about?"
"Your mother said…."
"Oh so Joann's still spinning that tale is she? It's been years since I heard that one."

"What do you mean? I held my breath as I waited for her to speak. Please, please, please.
"She's not mine, she's Joann's."
"That's it Joann Fielding, that's who I met..." Vito had finally figured it out.

Chapter 13

CHASE

This shit was getting confusing. I looked over to Delia and she was looking just as bewildered as I was. I didn't appreciate the fact that Celine was laughing either. Roomful of people or not, I would slap that bitch into next fucking month if I didn't get some answers in the next five minutes.

"What do you mean she's Joann's, why would she lie?"
"Why should I tell you anything, what's in it for me?"
"Your life. If you tell me what I want to know without anymore bullshit lies and theatrics I won't break your fucking neck and bury you out back."

She looked around the room as if seeking a defender but no one was buying. "You wouldn't dare. Delia are you going to let him treat me like that?"
"I...."

"Not another word Delia." I kept my eyes on my prey because sure as shit I would break her neck no problem. I'd had enough of the bullshit between her and her lying ass apparently slut of a mother.

"You don't talk to her, you talk to me. She doesn't exist for you anymore, your days of using her and your family fucking with her are long gone, now start talking, my patience is wearing thin."

She huffed and tried to play it off, but either the high was wearing off and she needed another fix, or she realized that I wouldn't think twice about ending her pathetic life, or at the very least maiming her ass.

"Whatever, it's like he said." She flung her hand in Vito's direction. "We never met."
"Why would your father go along with such a lie if it weren't true?"

"Because he doesn't know." She smirked again and came to within an inch of getting gut punched.
"Come again, how's that possible?"

"Because he wasn't here, he was away in the army, desert something." She scrunched up her face as if giving it some thought.

"And...."

"And Joann went bar hopping and ended up with some guy that knocked her up. When she realized that there was no way to pass the thing off as my dad's she concocted this scheme to pass it off as mine." She shrugged her shoulders like it was nothing.

"You call her a thing one more time, or say anything derogatory about her and I'll get the information another way. How far do you want to try and push me to see if I would really break your fucking pathetic neck?"
She took a step back from my advance.

"Why did you go along with it?"
"It got me my freedom, dad was a freaking nightmare. You can't do this you can't do that, but with Joann in my pocket I had my get out of jail free card."

"And your treatment of Delia?"
"Joann hates her because of the simple fact that she exist. I think the only reason she didn't get rid of it...I mean her." She corrected herself when I made to reach for her neck.

"Go on...."

"I think by the time she found out she was pregnant it was too late to get an abortion, so she had to have her."
"How did she pass her off as yours?"

"That was easy, she took me out of school. The story was that I was too distraught by my father's deployment so I was to be homeschooled. Joann wore baggy clothes and shit, did most of her food shopping in the next town over; we pulled it off. Then when it was time to give birth we went to this midwife out in the boondocks, and voila. I became the proud mother of a bouncing baby girl."

"And Carl never suspected."
"By the time he came home she was already three months old. Joann never breastfed, she'd gotten her body back in shape, so there was no need for him to suspect anything. He was sure pissed though, but Joann kept him off my back."

"Where did the story of Mr. Escalante raping you come in?"

"Oh, that was all Joann. She figured that if dad thought I was raped he wouldn't blame me, and she chose him because he's the one who knocked her up. She didn't think he would remember her since he was some type of player back then, and besides, she begged dad not to pursue it, not to bring shame and scrutiny to the family. She said since they were so wealthy they would use their wealth and influence to paint me as the guilty party, that I somehow duped him."

"Are we done? Because I really need to go." She was rubbing her arms up and down as if she were cold.
"The story checks out partially so far. She was out of school for thirteen months; Carl was in Kuwait...."Drew was busy on his computer. I didn't even want to know how he had access to this sort of information.

"What about the birth certificate?"
"Joann signed it. I think she told dad she did it to keep the stigma off of me. She made him believe that it was me who gave birth in the old hut and that she took me to the hospital later and had me sign her name." Another shrug.

I was only interested in one thing. I went over to Delia and knelt down in front of her. Drawing her close, I whispered so only she could hear.

"Did you hear that baby, she's not your mom. I know that was bothering you so could you please stop stressing over it now? Give little peanut a break okay."

She nodded and clung to me, her body a lot less tense than it was before. "Thank you Chase."
"You're welcome baby."
"So you mean...she's mine?" I'd almost forgotten the other people in the room until Vito spoke.

"It looks that way, if you'd like to have proof...." I didn't really know what was to become of this. If one more person rejected or belittled her worth I was gonna lose my shit.

"No, no, no, that won't be necessary, she's her aunty Tessa all over again. I don't need anything else to tell me she's mine, besides like I said, I remember meeting this Joann woman all those years ago, more than once. But she never said...."

He turned to look at Delia. I guess all that he'd heard so far was replaying in his head as he put the pieces of the puzzle together. I'll have to fill him in a little later.

This time when he walked over to Delia I didn't try to stop him. He stood right in front of us, just staring at her with a longing expression on his face.

"I didn't know, had I known I would've come for you. I promise, I didn't know...Maxwell." My father came and led the big strong man with tears in his eyes from the room.

"And once again she lands on her feet. How could an unwanted piece of garbage have so many fucking lives?" I wasn't quick enough to stop Delia as she flew across the room and slapped her sister across the mouth.

"That's for trying to hurt my baby." Celine had a scared look on her face as she held her bruised cheek and drew back. Okay then. Delia turned and came back to me with a scowl on her face. I guess she was too pissed to put together all that was going on around her right now, like the fact that she had a new father.

My mind was going sixty miles a minute. If Vito Escalante accepted her as his daughter, which looked more than possible knowing my godfather. She had just become the heiress to a fortune that could rival mine. And the daughter of one of the most powerful men in the country if not the world. Celine has no idea.

Chapter 14

CHASE

When Vito and dad came back to the room, he was a bit more composed. I can't begin to imagine what it must feel like to a man who had believed he would die childless, to find out at his age that he had an almost adult daughter. He must be in a state of shock.

He gave Delia a long look before turning to Celine, who was now sitting on the floor rummaging through her bag looking for who knows what.

"Young lady, I need some answers and since you seem to be the only one here with any insight into my daughter's life I'll be asking you...."

"I'm all talked out, unless there's something in it for me. After all why should she reap all the benefits?"

"While my young godson threatened to break your neck, I assure you, my punishment for you would be much more severe. Maxwell has filled me in on some of what you and your delightful family have done to her so far. I wouldn't break your neck, for what you've done to my daughter, I would have you tortured before I fed you to my dogs, do not fuck with me. Excuse me Delia and Rhina." He bowed his head in apology to the two ladies like the gentleman he was.

Celine spluttered all over her face, but in the end self preservation kicked in and the whole story came pouring out. She talked about how she used Joann's fear of discovery against her, making sure neither Joann nor Carl ever showed one ounce of affection to the new baby.

How She played on her father's guilt for not being there when his little girl was supposedly raped. The more she spoke the more I wanted to be sick. Vito looked like he wanted to kill her and Delia was crying her heart out, while my family was deathly still.

No one moved as the ever-mercenary little bitch told her tale with hardly any inflection or emotion in her voice. When she spoke of how she went out of her way to make Delia's life a living hell I thought I would really snap and end the bitch.

There was a commotion out in the hallway before whoever was there rushed into the room. Santino and Rocco Escalante came into the room. Both men were a few years older than their brother. Santino was the eldest of the three, with Rocco two years behind.

"Where is she?" Santino spoke, his eyes searching the room until he lit on Delia. I guess Vito had given them a heads up while he'd left the room earlier.

"Oh my...Rocco...." He grabbed for his brother's arm before they both made their way towards Delia and I. They studied her from head to toe, taking in every aspect of her features before Santino stepped forward.

"Hello little Delia, I am your uncle Santino, and this is your uncle Rocco."
"Hello, pleased to meet you." Her voice was small and tired. I think the events of the day were finally catching up to her as she shook hands with her uncles.

"Well Vito, fill us in."
They both took a seat as Vito filled them in on what we had learned so far. They were none too happy to hear about the poor treatment of their niece to say the least.

There was bantering back and forth about what action should be taken. I always knew my godfather and his brothers had reputations for being cutthroat in the business world, but I'd never known them to be vengeful, tonight I was learning a new lesson.

I listened as everyone had an opinion on what needed to be done at this point, if anything. Rocco was trying to figure out how to bring charges against Joann and Carl, but for what? Santino kept his silence but he was thinking very hard while doing it.

This went on for some time until the talk turned to other matters, namely Delia's place in their family.

"Of course we have to change everything. Those bungling idiots that have been chomping at the bit waiting to pick over our carcasses aren't going to be too happy." Santino cackled at his own humor.

My mom who had left the room without me noticing came in with a tray of refreshments. I forced Delia to have some juice and a sandwich even though she protested that she wasn't hungry. She'd been following the conversation between her father and his brothers with wide eyes. I just held her close. I didn't think now was a good time to tell her their worth. It just might be the straw that broke the camel's back.

"Think of the baby, it's been a while since peanut ate anything and you know that's no good for her." I thought I'd spoken softly enough that only she heard but I underestimated how deeply engrossed in her Vito was.

"Baby, a baby...." Vito was across the room in a flash, taking her hands in his. "I'm going to be a grandfather?"
"Who the fuck cares, somebody get me out of here, I need to go...."

"Who is this vile creature?" Oh shit I had forgotten all about the drugged out whore on the floor. It looked like she'd taken a nap sitting up against the wall.

"That's the sister." Vito offered.

"Oh is it?" Oh hell, Santino looked...what the fuck is that look? I don't think I've ever seen it on a human being outside a movie. Sinister was too tame a word.

I had the feeling the Fieldings were in for a world of hurt, and if they thought I was bad, even I knew I had nothing on the Escalantes. I felt myself shiver as the three brothers turned their attention on Celine.

Damn, she's so fucked.

Chapter 15

DELIA

Well it looks like I have a new father. I'm not quite sure what's going on around me, everything seems to be going really fast and I can't seem to catch up. After Vi...my...father stopped going on about the baby things had gone something like this.

"Well now she must come home with us."
"Uh, no. I respect how you feel, you've just met your long lost daughter, you're excited about that understandably, but my wife stays with me, always, no exceptions."

There was silence following that mandate by Chase. No one spoke for a while. I drew closer to him and accepted his reassuring squeeze. He didn't seem too worried about the outcome so I relaxed against his side. As much as I wanted to explore this new family dynamic of mine there was no way I was leaving him to do it.

"Okay boys, let's go." Vito summoned his brothers and they rose from their chairs to leave. "Where are you going godfather?"
"You'll see soon enough not to worry daughter we'll be back." With that they were gone.

Chase and I had spent another hour with his family before he decided it was okay to take me home to our own fortress. Cue eye roll. I had the feeling it might be some time before I saw the outside world again.

We were both a little jolted when the three brothers showed up an hour later on our doorstep with their suitcases. Chase just shook his head, opened the door wider and pointed up the stairs.

"You know where everything is."
They bounded up the stairs like three teenagers instead of the middle aged men they were.

***

That was three days ago and now I find myself, hiding out. If I thought having to deal with Chase's over protectiveness was a pain, it was nothing compared to the tyranny of my new father and uncles; now instead of one overbearing male I had to contend with four.

It had been decided that I wouldn't go back to school for a while, that had caused the first argument. The brothers thought I should go to a top-notch university to learn the ins and outs of business. My father thought he should just hire someone to teach me the ropes, and Chase said I will do whatever I chose to do as long as we didn't have to be separated.

How something like that could go on and on for hours, was beyond me but I soon learned that the brothers liked to argue with each other.

They fell over each other trying to boss me around. Chase thought it was funny, he could go off to the office knowing that no one was getting anywhere near me with my new guardians on the job. He said he had the best of both worlds. Our bedroom was far enough away that we could still get as loud as we wanted to so our sex life was in no way hindered, and he had someone or ones to run rough shod over me while he was at work. Huh.

"Chase, you have to make them stop." He laughed on the other end of the line.
"Why, what are they doing now?"

"They got ahold of one of your crazy books that says its good for the baby if I eat all natural foods while in the womb. Now they're juicing and baking from the pulp or some such thing. The only problem is they wouldn't let me help and I don't think any of them have ever seen the inside of a kitchen in their lives."

He laughed his fool head off but I was being very serious. I don't think I've been allowed to lift anything heavier than a fork since they got here.

I'd asked if they didn't have to go to work and they'd looked down their noses while admonishing me that men of their worth didn't work, as much as they oversaw their dynasties.

When they started talking about my having to meet with their moneymen and board members and whatnot I got a headache. I could barely grasp the concept of Chase's wealth and largesse after coming from such humble beginnings. Accepting that I was now the heir to not only my father's but my uncles' fortunes was just too out there.

I'd asked if they didn't have anyone else, no other family member that was expecting to inherit, but they had planned to leave their wealth to a committee that would feed certain charities and other interests they had after they were gone. They were only too happy to give it all to me. It was too much.

Chase said I'll get use to the idea in time but I wasn't too sure. As for my other family, there was something in the works there but no one was telling me anything. In the evenings Maxwell and Drew would come over and the men would lock themselves away, while Rhina and I sat talking or knitting baby booties. I would beg for leniency but Chase's face always got hard when I tried and my father and uncles just patted my head and told me it was nothing for me to worry my head about. They scared me.

Celine had been escorted from the Thornton residence by some men that the Escalante brothers had called all hush-hush. She'd screamed and cursed a blue streak, but those guys made the secret service look like puppets, no expression on their faces not even a twitch.

I didn't even try listening in at the door because Chase had promised to tan my hide if he ever caught me doing that. When I reminded him about the baby he told me there were ways around that, I stayed away.

When I didn't show much interest in their vendetta against Joann and Carl he said it was okay because he had enough hatred for both of us. I wish he would listen to me. I know he thought he was doing this for me, but he doesn't realize he had already given me more than I'd expected out of this life.

He'd given me himself, his love, his care, our child and now this. A whole new family who saw me so differently from the other, they really loved me. So was it fair for me to be hiding away from them when all they were doing was showing me that love?

"I'm going to help them make a mess, I'll force them to let me help."
"Go get 'em tiger." I walked into the kitchen a few minutes later not quite sure what I'd find.

"Ah, there she is, come sit here child." Santino pulled out a chair for me. I tried to ignore the orange liquid splashed over every available surface on the island, or the line of carrot pulp that led from one end to the other.

"What are you doing uncle?"
"We're making carrot muffins from this book." He looked at the book like it was a snake. His two accomplices were arguing measurements over a bowl that had flour and sugar in it.

"How about I read it off and guide you guys. I won't move a muscle I promise."
"Splendid idea, she gets that from me." My father gloated. I think he liked to rub it in that he was the one with a daughter and a grandchild on the way, but the other two didn't seem to take offense.

"I say Tessa sent her, or came back or something, because she's all of Tessa. We have such stories to tell you about your aunt, such a sweet girl." Rocco got melancholy and teary eyed.

I knew that they'd had a sister who died when she was very young from pneumonia. They'd shown me pictures and I have to say, there wasn't much difference. Had I not known I myself would've thought someone had snapped a photo of me unawares. "I can't wait to hear all about her."

And so it began again they talked over each other trying to be the first to tell me. Arguing some point or the other, trying to one up each other. I could only laugh, after all Chase had told me these men were cutthroat scions of the business world. Who would believe it of them in their kiss the cook aprons?

Chapter 16

CHASE

I'm extremely happy for Delia, her and her new- found family. My godfather and honorary uncles has made me so proud, the way they so readily accepted her. Thank heaven she looked like her aunt that made the need of any blood tests unnecessary. It was good that they accepted her without question although her mother was a chronic lying bitch.

Delia on the other hand had insisted that they have the test done and it was only yesterday they'd gotten the results back. No surprise there, she was without a doubt most definitely his.

The three nuts that had taken up residence in our house thought this was an excuse to throw a party. Poor Delia was knee-deep in party planning with my mom, Paulina and a party planner. A party in her honor was a novelty to her and she was in turns excited and overwhelmed.

I kept on top of her, making sure she didn't overdo, because when the Escalante brothers weren't overseeing their empire they were busy driving my wife crazy.

She'd already started meeting with their henchmen as she called them. Every morning as I was leaving, their goons in suits would be at the door ready to stretch her poor brain with all she needed to know to take over the vast holdings. Hopefully that won't be for many years to come.

It was a jump for someone who'd been studying to be a schoolteacher. She was a trooper though and these days, it was hard to find the girl who'd been so beaten down by life and the people around her.

In her place is a beautiful, vibrant woman who shone, who owned her husband heart and soul. This afternoon I'm stealing her away for some one-on-one time. She was flourishing under their care along with my family's love and affection, but it felt like I haven't been alone with my wife in forever. And even though our sex life hadn't really suffered any, I was feeling selfish. I miss having her all to myself.

So I'd stolen her away, just leaving them a note letting them know she was with me. Instead of heading to the condo I went instead to a hotel. Room service sounds good right about now.

My baby was all excited to have her man to herself for the first time in weeks. All the way there, in the car, she clung to me, her head on my shoulder.

"You okay there baby girl?"
"Uh huh, just can't wait to be alone with my daddy." I kissed her forehead when we stopped for the light.
"You not overdoing it are you?"

"Please, I'm dying of boredom. Those three old men are worse than women. They pamper me all day like I'm an invalid. I'm not allowed to go up and down the stairs I have to take my afternoon nap which apparently is a prerequisite for all pregnant women oh excuse me 'women in the family way', on the couch. I'm fed every couple hours; they make you seem very tame in comparison.

"I'm feeling a little jealous here."
"No need, you're the best husband in the world." She squeezed my arm.
"Thanks baby."

We checked in at the front desk where I almost slapped the shit out of the kid working there. He was eyeing my fucking wife like she was the last piece of pie and he was starving.

"Do you mind?" I scowled darkly at the little shit.
"Uh, sorry sir...um here's your key card sir enjoy your stay." His face flushed as I continued glaring at him.

Delia pulled on my arm to move me away before I knocked some manners into his ass.
"Chase, he wasn't even really checking me out. I'm an old pregnant married woman now remember?"
"You're fucking hot and you know it."
"Only you think that Chase no one else ever has, only you."

"I don't believe that for a second. I think you just weren't paying attention." Plus the fact that her family had her believing that she was less than nothing. Now with her newfound confidence and that special glow about her, she was even more beautiful than ever.

There's nothing sexier to a man than a confident woman. My girl's well on her way to being fully confident, which meant I'd have to think of ways to repel mother fuckers like that snot nosed kid at the desk.

In the room I picked her up in my arms nuzzling her, just happy to be holding her in my arms. Happy, that I could share in her joy, happy that we were having a baby together just fucking happy.

I didn't let thoughts of her family intrude. Things were being set in motion to deal with them. Santino and surprisingly enough, Rocco, had opted to kill the three remaining Fieldings. They weren't kidding either. Me, I could go either way and that was the honest truth.

Dad, ever the clearheaded one brought reason to the table and so they continue to live...for now.
"Do you want to eat first baby, relax in the Jacuzzi, what do you want to do, it's up to you?"

"No, I just want to be with you. How long are we here for?"
"The whole night, we can make it two if you'd like."
"You have work."

"Nope, dad has it all under control. Though I think your father and uncles might put out an APB on us."

She pulled her sweater over her head as soon as I put her back on her feet. The new fullness to her breasts was mouth watering. I watched her undress down to the little pink bikini panties she wore.

"Leave those."
I helped her remove my clothes until I stood before her naked and erect Pre cum already flowing in anticipation.

"Touch me." She took me in her hand and stroked, making me draw in my breath. I pushed my hips forward, enjoying the feel of her soft hand wrapped tightly around my cock.

Pushing my hand inside her panties, I grabbed her ass cheek and squeezed before caressing her pussy slit with the barest touch of my fingers.

"Uhmmm." She pushed back against my fingers. I licked her mouth before taking it in a hot kiss that had her climbing to her toes.

I sat her on the edge of the bed and had her lay back legs opened wide, before kneeling on the floor in front of her. "Play with your clit while I eat your pussy babygirl." Her hand went to her pussy and she started diddling her clit while I watched and stroked my own meat.

I stuck my tongue out and licked just inside her, making her hiss. Our eyes held as I pleasured her with my mouth, fucking her with my tongue until she screamed and came.

"How do you want me?"
She turned over on her hands and knees, her ass in the air, pussy glistening, just begging to be fucked. I eased into her listening for that little sound she makes every time I enter her.

Holding her upper thighs in my hands I sawed in and out of her as she grabbed the sheets, her pussy already weeping all over my raging cock. With feet planted firmly on the floor I stroked into her deeply, running my hand down her spine to her ass.

"You're getting better at taking me this way." I was going all the way in with ease as she fucked back at me. We stayed slow and easy through her first two orgasms and then the pounding started. Leaning over her back, I took her breasts in my hands as I alternated between pounding and grinding my dick into her.

"Fuck, I want to cum in your ass."
She laid her head flat against the bed, reached back with both hands and pulled her ass cheeks apart for me. I pulled out of her pussy and entered her ass. Her juices and mine combined to make it an easy entry.

"I love fucking your sexy ass." She keened and pushed back as I reached around and put two fingers inside her pussy, she covered my hand with hers, guiding me at the pace she needed to reach climax.

"Chase, ooh...I'm cumming...uhmmmmmm...."
The tingling started in my head and travelled to my toes before I emptied my load in her ass, grunting and jerking as I was spent.

I kissed her as my now deflated cock slipped out of her ass, my sperm leaking out of her.

"Two nights." That was my dictate as I left her in the bed to go run us a bath.

Chapter 17

CHASE

At the end of our second night together, we returned home the following morning to a house of madness. I wasn't sure if it was the Three Stooges or the Three Musketeers that had taken up residence, but as soon as we set foot in the house Delia was confiscated, and I was given the stink eye.

I just shook my head, kissed my wife with a 'good luck' and headed upstairs with our luggage. Poor thing, she was begging me with her eyes to save her, but I knew what was coming in the days ahead, so I let her enjoy the pampering they were about to shower her with.

Later that evening, after Delia had taken about as much as she could, I snuck her upstairs and put her to bed.
"You had a long day huh baby!"
"I'm fine." She stretched before settling down.

Fuck! I needed to get downstairs. The Escalantes were waiting for me to discuss the next step in dealing with the Fieldings, but she looked so warm and soft and...ripe.

Her pregnancy showed mostly in her breasts, which were about to spill out of the little number she was wearing, my dick was standing at attention. Greedy!

We'd spent the last two days in bed, hardly ever leaving it. We didn't even leave to eat, settling instead for room service, and here I was, ready to ravish my sweet girl again.

"Kisses." I teased my nose across hers playfully.
She held her arms up to clasp around my neck as I lowered my lips to hers. My hands automatically went around her middle, pulling her body up to mine as I sucked her tongue into my mouth.

"Hmmmmmm, baby you need to rest."
"Okay."
She still didn't release her hold on my neck.
I pulled back and passed my fingers gently over her eyes as I laid her back against the pillows.
"Sleep." One last kiss and I left her.

The brothers were already sitting around the study with their snifters of brandy, seemingly in the middle of a heated discussion. Well Santino and Rocco were anyway Vito was his usual silent watchful self.

"Santino, we've been all over this already and it's been decided that we must act in a civilized manner." Rocco took a sip of his brandy after admonishing his brother.

"From what we've gathered so far, they weren't very civil to our girl in her formative years."
“I'm getting pretty tired of hearing about this civilized shit. We all know Maxwell has always been a gentleman, maybe we can take them out and just not tell him."

He seemed so excited by the idea.
I rolled my eyes as I took my seat in the last available chair, dad wouldn't be joining us tonight.

I wasn't so green that I didn't know why. Out of all of us, dad was the only one staunchly against outright taking out the Fieldings. He'd made his feelings on the subject known and I guess he figured there was nothing left to be said.

I myself had lost a little bit of my blood lust; she was safe now. She had love and acceptance. I no longer had a burning desire to choke the fucking life out of the three remaining Fieldings, but I sure as hell intended to make them pay still.

I hadn't eased up on my campaign to destroy them. The last report had them selling their cars and Celine's along with some other pricier things that they couldn't afford to begin with, in order to make a payment on the called in loan.

Joann was busy trying to do damage control with the whole Country Club thing and to top it all off, they had no idea where Celine was.

Joann and Carl also had no idea that Delia had found her father, since Celine was hidden away somewhere drying out in the worst way possible. We'd thought it prudent to keep her from spilling the beans until we came up with a plan. I guess you had to get your licks in wherever you could.

I knew from a medical standpoint, that withdrawal from hard drugs was not an easy thing, and to endure them without medical assistance was torture. Vito was not fucking around, and they'd only just begun.

"This is what we're going to do." Vito finally joined the discussion.
"I want all three players in the room together. I want to judge the man's reaction to these things. It could be that he's innocent of knowing of his wife's perfidy, though he might be guilty of neglecting my daughter. But let's not forget, he was under the misconception that Delia is the product of his young child's rape. In all things we must be fair."

"What about the jackal and her spawn?"
"That, is an entirely different matter Santino, they will be dealt with accordingly."

"I don't want Delia knowing about any of this...."
"We know that son, and that's another thing we must consider, she has such a soft heart it might do more damage than good if we brought death to her family."

"So what're you saying, we should let them get away with this shit?" He gave Santino an arched look, that seemed to be all the answer the brother needed as he sat back and took a swig of his drink with a small smirk on his face.

"No my brother, but I'm thinking that death might be too easy for them. There are some fates worse than death, much worse...Think of it, if we kill them Delia is the only one who will suffer, as the only remaining one left behind to grieve them, they do not deserve her grief. Also, she'd have to live with knowing that the men of her family had their blood on their hands, another blow."

"No, I think she's suffered enough. As long as we establish that she will no longer have any dealings with the Fieldings ever again, then we can commence with their...retribution."
I wouldn't want to be on the other end of that sinister smile.

Chapter 18

CHASE

It's amazing how fast time passes when you're plotting the demise of assholes. By the wee hours of the morning we'd mapped out a course of action that was acceptable to everyone.

It was done with my wife's best interest at heart of course, the only problem was, I wanted to keep Delia as ignorant of the goings on as possible and to do that I might have to send her away.
I wasn't feeling that shit at all.

The only other option was to let her in on what we had planned. I wasn't too sure how she'd take any of this. On the one hand, I didn't want to have any secrets between us, on the other I don't want her experiencing one moments' guilt over those three fucks.

In the end it was decided that I'll sleep on it, but as soon as I gave the word it would be a go. Delia had already made her feelings on the matter known. I wish I could give her-her wish, but I'd seen first hand what they'd done to her, how they'd belittled her, torn her down. Just thinking about it pissed me the fuck off so no, I wasn't about to just let shit slide.

I stayed awake for a long time with Delia wrapped securely in my arms, as I tried to come up with the best solution. Though I know I would do pretty much anything to make her happy, I couldn't give her this one thing. The protector in me just couldn't let it go.

I'll have to make it up to her somehow but they were going to pay dearly for what they'd done...and I'm going to discuss it with her, no scratch that, I'm going to tell her.

With the decision finally made, I found it easier to fall asleep. I woke up the next morning to a nice surprise. I must've been really out of it because I didn't feel any of the build up. I just opened my eyes to my wife riding me, her head thrown back, breast pressed together between her arms, which were planted on my stomach.

The look of immense pleasure on her face was indescribable. It's almost as if she'd gone off into her own little world, just using my dick for her pleasure. Her teeth biting into her bottom lip as she rocked back and forth.

The little grunting noises she made each time she came down on my cock were unbelievably sexy. I watched her for a moment, just fascinated by her and what she was doing, enjoying the view of her ripening body. The slight mound of her tummy, the heated flush to her skin. The way her nipples jutted as if begging for my touch.

Raising my hands, I took her breasts, pinching her nipples. Her eyes flew open in surprise. She looked almost startled to be caught until I smiled at her. "Is this okay?" She didn't stop moving as she asked me that question. I don't think she could've.

"It's very okay." I pushed her hair back behind her ears as I pulled her down to me so I could feast on her hot skin. I bit into her neck, licking the spot to soothe it, before sucking my way down to her nipple. Her body picked up speed as I tongued her nipple and teased her swollen clit with my thumb.

"Cum for me baby, I wanna fuck you." I growled into her ear as my body thrust up into hers. She clenched around my cock tighter at my harshly spoken words.

It thrilled the fuck out of me that my innocent little girl liked dirty talk. If I wanted to bring her off in a hurry, all I had to do was whisper hot, nasty secrets in her ear and she went off like a rocket.

"Do you want your husband to pound your sweet little pussy, huh, would you like that?"
"Uh huh." Her hips were going crazy as she ground herself down harder on my cock.

"How do you want to be fucked? doggie style or with your legs over my shoulders huh? You want me to finger fuck that tight little ass while I fuck you babygirl, huh?"

She came on a scream, her head falling to my chest as her pussy clenched around my cock. Before the last tremor left her body I turned her over onto her back and taking her mouth with mine I drove into her.

Our mouths clashed as I bit into her lip softly, running my tongue over her teeth before giving it to her to suck. I fucked her mouth with my tongue, trying to consume her, to draw her into me.

"Not close enough...never close enough." Pulling out I covered her with my mouth, my tongue going straight into her, her juices running into my mouth and down my chin.

I licked her pussy until she begged me to fuck her. My cock was only too happy to oblige. We fucked in a frenzy, our bodies slapping together, the sounds loud in the room.

With her legs over my arms I deep stroked into her wet pussy as she moaned for me as her eyes rolled back in her head. I needed to be deeper in her. I felt the urge to taste her flesh in my mouth so I bit her, right over her breast, making her scream and cum on my cock again.

"Fuck Delia, fuck me...so good." I didn't want it to end, didn't want to leave the haven of her sweet body. I could stay balls deep in her forever and never grow tired.

"Look at me." I pulled her head back as I continued to piston my hips back and forth, driving myself deeper still into her. "You're mine, you'll always be mine. I'll never stop wanting you, never."

Her mouth opened as if to speak but her words got stuck in her throat as I once again took her tongue into my mouth for a little love play. I felt my cock lengthen as my balls tightened up against my body, my pace quickened as I raced towards climax.

"Cum beautiful girl, cum for me." I took the choker around her neck that said I owned her between my teeth as I poured my seed inside her.

"Fuck baby, that was amazing, thank you." I kissed her, little pecks until her heart rate settled. "What were you dreaming about that made you attack me?" I teased her playfully as I brought her into my arms.

"Nothing, he was poking me in my butt like he wanted me to come out and play." She hid her face in my chest and I just knew she would be blushing.

"You can play with him anytime you want sweetheart, he's yours." She looked up with a smile and kissed me. We'd come such a long way in such a short time. All the love and devotion we felt for each other seemingly miraculous.

I'd started out on the road to revenge and found instead my greatest treasure; something I in no way deserved. Her precious innocence, her sweetness of heart, the way she accepted me, loved me, it blows my mind. And then....

"How's our baby?" I placed my palm over my little princess in the womb.
"Peanut is quiet this morning."
"Maybe we should start every day like this, it'll go a long way to making my day a good one and if it keeps her little ass quiet all the better."

"You have to go to work today huh!"
"And you have to get back to the grindstone Miss businesswoman."

"Hah, businesswoman, that's rich. That whole thing is so intimidating but yet they seem to think I should just be able to pick it up. According to uncle Santino, it's in the blood, my father tries to be patient but I can tell he wants me to know everything yesterday. Uncle Rocco is the only one who seems to want to give me time. Though he usually pats me on the head and says,' not to worry little Del, you'll get it soon enough.' But seriously, can't I come to work with you? I could help out at the front desk, I won't be any bother I promise."

I laughed at her forlorn face and with a kiss to her brow I tried to reassure her. "I'll tell your crazy relatives to tame it down a little. They don't mean to drive you crazy, it's just that...you're a part of them, a part that had been missing for a very long time. I think they're trying to make up for lost time, not to mention the circumstances of your upbringing, they feel a little guilt over that."

"But why, they didn't know, how could they have stopped it?"
"It's not that easy baby, they're powerful men. Men like that hate feeling like they've failed, add the fact that you look so much like their long lost sister and the guilt is only intensified."

"But I don't want them to feel guilty." My soft girl sounded close to tears. Was it any wonder I wanted to destroy those who'd done her harm? How could I not want to avenge one so perfectly precious?

"Ssh, it's okay, time will take care of that I think, but...there's something else...."

I didn't say anything else for a while suddenly not too sure. This being in love shit is a whole new world, usually I could give a fuck, so what someone else thought didn't matter too much to me. With Delia I cared too much so I found myself weighing every decision, trying to choose what was best for my wife.

"What, what is it?" She lifted her head from my chest and looked at me.
"We've decided what to do about your family." I said it in one long breath and then I held my breath as I felt her body tighten against me.

Chapter 19

CHASE

I spent the next hour trying to explain things to her but she wasn't quite there yet. "But she's still my mom."
"No, no she's not, don't give in to some melancholic make believe dream here baby. You and I both know that she was never a mother to you, not in any sense of the word."

She started crying again, which was in no way helping her case. For every tear that fell, I was going to fuck them over even worse.

Eventually I took the reins back, with her head clasped between my hands, I looked into her wet eyes.
"You don't have to do anything okay love, none of this is your fault." I put my hand on her stomach.

"Would you let harm come to her?"

"Of course not." She hiccupped through her answer.
"If someone tried to harm me in any way...." She got the meanest look I'd ever seen on her little face before I could even finish the sentence.

"Ah, ah, ah, you see, do you see how you feel with just the thought of someone hurting me? Well I saw them hurt you Delia, a lot, how do you think I feel? Do you think you love me any more than I love you? Do you think I mean more to you than you do to me? Not possible sweetheart. I won't let them get away with what they did to you. I know you don't understand and that's okay for now but they must pay. Do you know I was willing to let things go?"

She looked at me skeptically, but I ignored that, she knew her husband was a vengeful sort.

"I was going to try to respect your wishes and let things slide. But then Celine hurt you and they hid her whereabouts. It didn't matter to them that my innocent child could've been harmed all they cared about was protecting their precious fucked up daughter. Well your father, uncles, and especially your husband wants to show them that you're no longer what they tried to make you. You're loved and cherished...no-no don't cry beautiful girl it'll be alright you'll see." I dried the tears that had fallen, wishing she'd never shed another over their undeserving asses.

"Everything's going to be fine babygirl, nothing's really going to change now is it? Besides, we have peanut to prepare for, we'll be too busy to think about anything else. Now all you need to do is stay happy and healthy. I don't want you worrying about any of this, it's not good for you and it's not good for our little peanut."

"But I won't see them...."

"Do you want to see them?" There was no way in hell she was going anywhere near them, not if I could help it. I just wanted her to come to the realization on her own that she didn't need them, that she was better off without them. Peanut for damn sure was never going to breathe the same air as them and she wouldn't be missing anything.

Between the Escalante brothers, my parents and her aunt and uncle, my little girl was going to be set for people to spoil her. Not to mention a father who couldn't wait to lavish her with love and everything her little heart desired. And Delia, well I just imagined she'd be the greatest mother to our little peanut. She had so much love in her after all how could she not be? Fuck the Fieldings.

"By the way, we never talked about you sneaking out of the house behind me that day and following me to their house. Don't do that again. I don't care what you think might be going on you don't go against my wishes, understood?"

"Yes...." Her voice was barely above a whisper.
"Okay now. I've told you what's going to happen, I'm not telling you this to get your approval, I'm telling you because I don't want a secret of this magnitude between us. These things have a way of coming back to bite you in the ass. With that said, we're going to go ahead and do it. I'm here if you need me, your dad and uncles are all here for support if you need it, but really I don't see the problem. At least we're letting the bastards live, after what they tried to do to you they're getting off easy. Now come here."

I pulled her onto my lap and held her close as I kissed her temple. "It's going to be okay, you'll see. It's not like I was even going to let you be around them ever again so you won't be missing anything anyway."
"But they'll suffer."

She didn't know the half of it. I'd shielded her from some of what had been planned, giving her just the bare facts. She didn't need to know the more ghastly details about what was going to befall those twisted wastes of fucking space.

Why she couldn't see them for what they are is beyond me, maybe she was too close to the situation. Whatever it was, I'm going to make sure and shield her from her own soft heart. I'm not too sure about Carl Fielding beyond the fact that he's a grade A ass for letting his wife and daughter manipulate him all these years and even going so far as to abuse an innocent, because that's exactly what their treatment of her was, abuse. He was the only one of the three I would have any compassion for if I were so inclined. Too bad for his sorry ass I'm not.
"Don't think about it baby."

***

I let things settle for a couple days. I didn't necessarily want her to know exactly when we were going to start our campaign of torture, so for the next two days it was business as usual. I went to work and she did whatever it is that she did when she was at home with the motley crew.

She seemed to be settling into the idea of running a corporation much easier these days. She was no longer intimidated it seemed and not surprisingly she did seem to have a head for it.

I had to put an end to the business quizzes when I got home in the evenings though, or the Escalantes would test her until it was time for bed, poor thing.

It was usually like taking my life in my hands when I interfered. To a man they would sneer at me and their argument was always the same. 'But she has so much to learn in such a short space of time.'

How the time got so short was beyond me. Just a few short weeks ago they didn't even have an heir, now it's like they wanted to run off into the sunset and leave her at the reins. I'm sure that wasn't the case but still, they acted like they expected her to be ready yesterday.

They were extremely excited to have found her and it showed. They'd moved into our damn house hadn't they? But they could stay as long as they want because the love she got from them went a long way to building up the girl who was always told she was nothing.

I'd just had to pull her out of their clutches again on the pretense of showing her something upstairs for which they were not thankful if the grumbles and sour looks were anything to go by.

"Thank you, my poor brain is about to leak out of my ears. Today's lessons were about international law and all it entails to run a business in other countries. I think I need another break, can't we run away again please?" She tried to con me with kisses. Perfect, just perfect.

"Why don't I have mom and Paulina take you out for a Spa day maybe some shopping?"
"Chase that sounds amazing. But have you ever been shopping with Paulina? She's a maniac. She'll drag us into every designer store in the city, then she'll make us try on stuff...grrrhh." She's so cute.

"I thought you liked that!" I laughed at her cute face.
"I do but...I'm hormonal I think."
"I know just what you need."

We barely got our clothes halfway off before I had her pinned beneath me. There was no foreplay, no build up. I just took my cock in hand and sank into her warm heat. We rocked back and forth gently as I whispered how much I loved her in between nibbles of her sweet lips.

"I love being inside you baby, it's the best feeling in the world." She clawed my back and sought my mouth with hers while her pussy twitched around my cock.

It was another long night spent buried inside her, but by morning the demise of her ex family wasn't foremost on her mind.

The following day she was none the wiser as my mom and sister came to pick her up for their girls' day out. She didn't question why I wasn't heading to the practice, or why dad and Drew were even here, since her father and uncles acted as though they had a perfectly innocent prearranged meet planned. As soon as the women cleared the driveway we were out the door.

We were meeting the men the Escalantes had set on Carl and Joann at the location where Celine had been kept all this time. I hadn't seen or even asked about her condition since they'd taken her away because I really didn't give a fuck.

To think I'd almost married that thing, damn. Life sure is strange. I'd stepped out of that frying pan and into a very nice fire.

The place was isolated. From the outside it looks like an abandoned warehouse; one of those old numbers with a million windows. There was overgrown grass in the cement cracks, and just a general sense of disuse.

The building was backed up to the woods so there was only one way in or out, and that was a well-hidden dirt track that couldn't be seen from the main road. In other words if you weren't looking for it, you'd never find it.

There were cars lined up in the lot around back as we pulled in and alighted. We'd all come together in my luxury SUV. More space, and we didn't want too much traffic. Somebody might notice all these strange cars going and coming from an abandoned building.

Major Fielding's raised voice could be heard as we entered the cavernous building. "Who are you people, do you know who I am, how dare you? Unhand me...Joann!"

Joann could be heard screeching like a scalded cat. The only one not heard from was Celine and I wondered if she was even cognizant. Oh well.

We entered the room silently and all movement stopped. I was the first one in so Joann went on the attack straight away.

"You...." She started to sneer at me until she got a good look at the other players filing into the room. She lost all color and stumbled back a step. "No!" Her hand went to her throat as she shook her head back and forth; good she was already afraid.

"Hello Joann, I'd say it was a pleasure, but that would be a blatant lie." Vito had that wolf on the hunt glare in his eyes.
"Who are you man?"
"Carl..."

Joann started but was silenced by a harsh, 'Quiet' from Vito, who seemed even more pissed off now that we were here and he was face to face with the woman who had so poorly mistreated his daughter. A daughter that he would've loved and cherished if given half a chance.

"Who are you?" The major repeated his question.

"Hello Major Fielding, I'm Vito Escalante, I'm told you've heard of me but we've never had the pleasure of meeting."

There was a derisive snort from the corner of the room where Celine sat looking nothing like her usual glamorous self. She looked like what she was a strung out junkie; stringy hair, scabby skin, and blotchy eyes that were swollen, and vacant.

"You, you're the one who raped my daughter you destroyed her life." He made as if to go after the other man, but was stopped short by the men who'd brought them in.

Vito held up his hand to halt the men. "That's why we're here today, to lay to rest that abominable lie. You see, I never laid eyes on your daughter until a little while ago."

"What...but...Celine?"
"Your daughter and your wife lied to you. You see, years ago while you were away serving your country, your darling wife was out trolling bars looking to get fucked, she found me. The girl you think is your granddaughter, the one you treated like an unwanted piece of lint is mine, mine and your wife's."

"What...Joann, what the hell is he talking about?"
"Carl I can explain let me explain."
"Explain what? Tell me that he's lying..." Celine started to laugh outright at this point.

"You're such a fucking sorry sap. Even now, faced with the truth you'd still believe her wouldn't you?" She shook her head as if he was a disappointment.

"Celine...you knew?...Of course you did, you two must've thought I was a fool all these years, beating myself up because I wasn't here to protect you when you were molested, all the guilt, you mercenary little bitch. And you, my dutiful wife...what have you done?"

"Oh give it up dad, you're trying to tell me you never once questioned that story, I mean did I even act like a mother towards that thing?"

One. Yep, I was keeping count of every thing she said against Delia, three strikes and I'd belt the bitch.
"I thought it was because she was the product of rape...I thought she was a bad reminder for you...I even treated her..." He turned to Joann.

"What kind of monster are you...what...how?"

This guy was too much even for me. He looked around the room as if searching for answers. Joann in the meantime was trying to disappear into the wall.

"Would you have ever told me the truth? Would I have died believing that the child was Celine's?"
"What difference does it make now? That was years ago. I've been loyal to you since then, it was only that one time, I was so lonely Carl can't you understand you'd been gone for...."

"I wasn't gone you filthy bitch I was off fighting a war and you were..." He looked like he was going to be sick. Celine meanwhile started up her laughing fit again. It almost seemed like she'd gone around the bend. In my practice I didn't have too much cause to deal with drug addiction or the side effects of drying out cold turkey so I just knew the barebones facts. But if I had to take a guess I would say its not for the faint of heart. Fuck she was a mess.

No one else in the room had spoken since the family farce had begun. Joann for once was left without a thing to say, then again, what could she say, faced with the truth as she was?

There was a roar of anger, followed by a blur of movement as Major Carl Fielding took the necessary steps to reach his wife. Before anyone had any idea of his intent, the major picked his wife up and chucked her out a window.

"What the fuck?" I didn't think he had it in him. Good, he'd done what my love for Delia kept me from doing.

Chapter 20

CHASE

"Well that's one way to handle it, though I think our idea was much more humane." Vito was cold as fuck as he walked over to the window.

The security team had already subdued a broken, sobbing Major Fielding, while his daughter looked on in a daze. I guess she figured she might be next so it was best to put crazy on hold.

Maybe they should release him so he could finish the job. I wouldn't mind one bit, three birds with one stone. Dad and I headed down the four flights of stairs while the others stayed behind. Already Drew was looking for a spin to give the authorities, that's my brother.

Her body was a twisted mess, there was blood already pooling around her. She groaned in misery as we approached, her neck at an odd angle. I knew what that meant.

"Help me...." The words garbled by the blood in her throat. Maybe the bitch would drown on her own blood. Dad gently turned her head slightly to avoid that happy occurrence. Oh well, she could always die from her injuries. I should be so lucky.

I looked down at her and couldn't find the human heart that I knew lived in me. Why should I care after the way she'd treated her own child? Even all these years later instead of coming clean, she'd still fed me that lie to save face. Almost destroying my wife in the process.

Fuck her, fuck her, fuck him and fuck her scuzzy drugged out mess of a daughter. I wish I could surround the building with gasoline and strike a match. After putting her back inside with the others of course.

The doctor in me wanted to help, the husband in me said fuck the bitch she got what she deserved.
"Let's get her out of here, I'll make the call." Dad took out his phone to call the paramedics.

Things had changed drastically, now we had a crime scene on our hands and there were going to be a lot of questions. Too bad we couldn't just bury all their asses in the back.

Dad made the call for the ambulance before kneeling down to take her hand in his. That's my father, compassionate to everyone, even those who'd shown none, me, not so much.

By the time the ambulance arrived with the police behind them, the Escalantes had had Celine spirited away. Her plight had always been planned to be separate from her parents, that was my call. The bitch had not only tried to cuckold me, but she'd gone after my wife and child, no fucking way she was getting away with it.

Fielding was out of our hands now I'm sure. If she survived he'd be charged with attempted murder, if she died, oh well. Either way works for me. A good ten or more years in jail was good enough payment for him, because although he might not have known the truth, he still contributed to her hell.

Anyone expecting me to feel an ounce of remorse for the day's events will be sorely disappointed. I wish he'd chucked both those bitches out the window and then maybe offed himself.

Okay I might have lied to my babygirl, just a little white lie. Though we had nixed the idea of killing them outright we'd certainly planned to make it easy for them to end up dead. Except for the major, we weren't quite sure how far his involvement went, so we weren't sure other than to make him suffer with the knowledge of his wife's betrayal how far to go.

We'd surmised that with her past coming back to haunt her and the threat of the community finding out, that Joann would take her own life. A narcissistic fuck like her wouldn't be able to live with the loss of respect even if they moved like we'd planned. Celine was another kettle of fish, the plans for her were still on course whether her accomplice lived or died.

The cops had a shit load of questions 'what were we all doing there?' etc. I wasn't too worried about their questions though, between my family and the Escalantes, there was no way anything was going to come of our presence here.

There were a handful of witnesses who'd seen Major Fielding throw his wife out the window. A good lawyer could claim duress, but I'm pretty sure the Escalantes would see that that didn't happen.

Needless to say it was a given that the major was going to spend some time behind bars. Doing hard time. It was hard to feel sorry for him. In this whole fucked up scenario there had been one victim, Delia, the innocent child who'd done nothing but had borne the brunt of a lie.

He was babbling like a two year old by the time they took him away in handcuffs. Our presence was simply explained as a family matter that revealed some harsh things; too much for the major to handle, and he reacted badly.

Delia's name was never mentioned and if I had my way, it never would be. That was the decision we'd all made before. That no matter what she'd had enough.

By three o'clock that evening, Joann had been stabilized. She would live but she'd never walk again. She'd spend the rest of her life dependent on others for her care. Let's hope her caregivers were as kind to her as she'd been to my wife. I would see to it.

As a doctor, I knew pretty much where all the worse places for the infirm could be found. And though we've always fought to put those places out of business, this time I was hoping for the worst for her. Words simply were not enough to describe how much I hated this woman.

From the hospital I headed to the ritzy hotel where Celine had been ensconced. I called my girl on the way to see how she was doing.

"Hi baby girl, how's your day so far?"
"Great, thank you so much, I can't believe how much I needed this, I got a massage and a facial and..."

"Whoa, whoa, whoa, slow down baby." She made me laugh. It felt good to laugh after the morning I'd had. I wish I could share with her what had transpired but no. We'll leave things as they were, letting her believe for at least a little while longer that her family had just been relocated somewhere.

Eventually I'd tell her the truth; then again maybe not. I didn't see the benefit in it for her. Vito and I had already pooled our considerable resources to ensure that none of this was ever leaked to the press. I didn't want her finding out some other way, not before I had a chance to tell her first, if ever.

"Oh, sorry, then I got lots of nice things for the peanut, wait until you see...." She went on and on about her day so far and all I heard was the joy, the lack of tension in her voice. I would do it all over again to ensure that she found this peace always.

No one else better fuck with her because I'd learned that I had no tolerance for anyone who did. She'd started out as...revenge I guess, and had become so much more. She was everything, she and peanut. I am going to spoil the hell out of them both. There wasn't anything she'd ever want for, first and foremost love. I'll make sure she had that everyday for as long as we lived. For everyday she'd gone without it I'd see she got double.

For all the heartache and misery she'd suffered as a child I would see to it that it was remedied tenfold. I will uncover every dream she's ever had, and if it was at all in my power, see to it that they came true.

"Baby, I want you to buy something...better yet let me talk to mom a minute." She passed the phone off to my mom. I could hear her and Paulina chattering away in the background.

"Hi son, what's going on?"
"Mom I need you to do me a favor."
"Anything!"
"I need you to buy Delia something totally frivolous and obscenely expensive. Don't let on what you're up to or she'll fight you tooth and nail, but if you should happen to be at the Jeweler's, or even one of those handbag places you like so much, if there's anything that she seems to like get it for her."

"That's my kind of favor, you're such a good kid."
"You raised me right I guess, let me say bye to my baby."
I said bye to her after telling her to have fun and that I'll see her later for dinner. Not one mention of her ex relatives, and I didn't feel any guilt, so far so good.

After I hung up, my whole attitude changed.

It was time to go face Celine for the last time. I didn't have much to say to her, besides she was so strung out it probably wouldn't mean much anyway. But I needed this closure, needed to put what she was behind me.

It's funny, throughout this whole ordeal I never once thought of what she'd done to me, not once. It was as though it didn't matter, but what she'd done to Delia, that deserved a hell of a lot worse than she was getting.

At the hotel the back door had been left slightly ajar as prearranged. I couldn't have it known that I was anywhere in the vicinity, that would raise way too many questions.

I slipped quietly up the stairway to the third floor, where the security cameras had been jammed to avoid my being caught on video.

The extra room key was where it was supposed to be, everything smooth and coordinated. The Escalante brothers are a little scary with their attention to detail, not to mention the way they command such loyalty from others.

She was already enjoying the goodies we'd had supplied for her and barely noticed the door opening.

"You, if it isn't the big bad Chase Thornton. How many lives are you planning to destroy today?"

I didn't bother answering her bullshit question. I was here for one thing only. "How are you doing Celine? You don't look so good."
"Screw you."
"No thanks, I like my dick exactly where it is. Besides, my wife is the most amazing lay I've ever had."

"That insipid bitch, hah." Her words were slurred and she was barely cognizant.
"I'll let that one slide." Yeah I was feeling generous because I could see our plan was working splendidly.

"Whatever, you two deserve each other anyway, losers."
"You didn't think I was such a loser when you were after me to marry you."

"That's because I thought you were fun..." She was busy getting high while we chatted. Was she always on drugs, or did she start down this path after the rehearsal dinner fiasco? I guess I'll never know.

I laughed my ass off at the fun reference but didn't reply, this wasn't about that anyway. I'd stopped beating myself up over her using me a long time ago. No, it was time to turn the screws and get the hell out of there. She was nothing, and looking at her here and now, her mask completely off and what she was plain to see, I was thankful once more that she'd not gotten her hooks in me.

"So anyway I'm just here to tell you about your sister and her good fortune. I'm sure you'd be happy to know that she is the heiress to a multibillion-dollar corporation, that her father and uncles are doing everything in their power to see that she's ready to run the corporation within a year. So now not only does she have my money and name behind her, she also has the Escalantes. She's now one of the wealthiest heiresses in the world."

I could just see the venom in her shooting eyes and tightened lips. Good, chew on that. I hope it's the last thing you think of before you draw your final breath.

"Did you know she's having our first child? Yep the first of many, even though you tried to kill this one with your little stunt, we plan to have at least six. All healthy boys and girls, who will be loved by their mother and father. Did I ever thank you for bringing my beautiful wife into my life? No? Sorry about that how remiss of me. Had I not met your lying deceitful ass I never would've found my treasure. She's the best thing to ever happen to me in my whole life, nothing else compares."

"Get out."
"Rot in hell you evil bitch." I didn't spare her one last look before turning for the door. That didn't take too long at all. She was fighting that needle into her arm pretty hard there by the end of my little speech.

I gave her at least two hours before she was gone. What else could you expect if you left a druggie in a room with an abundance of her drug of choice after so long drying out in the worst way possible? Not to mention the little nudge I'd just given her to help her on her way. See I didn't even have to touch her.

I could hear her through the closed door as I left. She was screaming and yelling profanity and threats against me Delia, and the whole world as I walked down the hallway. I walked away smiling.

Epilogue

Well, time has passed, as it is wont to do. I got my little peanut, Annabelle. She's just a few months old but she's already a spoilt princess.

The Escalante clan for all intents and purposes had taken up residence in our home, and I'm pretty sure that now with the baby here, it would take an act of the Almighty to get them out.

I have to literally fight to spend time with my wife and daughter. When it's not them, it's my own parents. My poor kid never has a moment to herself unless daddy confiscates her and hides out somewhere, which we both enjoy.

Delia is...flourishing, there's no other word for it. She's come a long way since we first met. She's still my sweet shy girl who needs her hubby-daddy to look after her, but she's cutting her teeth on one of her father's companies and really loving it. She shines.

Now the three nuts are talking about grooming my baby Belle to follow in their footsteps. I'm outnumbered and outgunned, but I'm grateful that they're here and that my wife gets to see first hand how much our daughter is loved.

She'd told me her fears one night after making love. Her fear that little peanut would grow up not feeling loved the way she had. I'd assured her that our daughter would have a vastly different upbringing than the one she'd suffered, but I guess in this case seeing is believing.

On weekends I hijack my little peanut before the rest of the house wakes up, put her on her mom's tit for her morning feeding while Delia is still between sleep and wake, and then we go for a drive.

That's our bonding time because I know for sure as soon as we get back to the asylum, she'll be snatched out of my arms and the three old women will start their fussing campaign.

At least I finally have my wife back. With all their fussing over the baby and their talk of missing out on Delia's childhood and making up for it with peanut, she was given a reprieve.

As to the little drama in our lives, things had pretty much settled down. Delia had eventually been told what had transpired, which led to one of our biggest arguments to date.

Not because she found fault with the way we handled things, but because she wanted to contact Carl and Joann. Celine as had been the plan had overdosed in that hotel room and wasn't found until a few days later, when the stench from her carcass had overpowered the guests on that floor.

I think the city buried her or something in pauper's field since she was pretty much beyond recognition and the name on the hotel sign in sheet was bogus. It was ruled an intentional suicide or some crap like that, who cares?

When Delia found out what Carl had done, and his guilt over the way he'd treated her-her whole life, my softhearted girl wanted to reach out to both of them, him and her incubator.

I was totally against it but as I found in the last year, it was hard to deny her anything. I knew Joann would take care of that for me anyway, the woman was extremely bitter and will always be.

The first time Delia had gone to see her she'd tried to spit on her. Even with her neck in a brace, paralyzed from the neck down, she'd tried to spit on her kid.

I'd been standing outside the door because there was no way I was going to let her go see that viper alone, but I had no interest in seeing that bitch ever again so I'd stayed just outside the door.

I'd dragged Delia out of the room quickly, after I'd heard Joann shouting obscenities at her. That was the first and the last time she'd been there.

As for Carl, he was an entirely different story. He was so full of remorse that I almost felt sorry for him, almost.

Dylan Thorpe and his bitch Maura had also found themselves at the end of a nasty campaign to get them out of town. What! Did you think I'd forget that they'd been part of the scheme to separate me from my money and make me a laughingstock?

Hell no. Last I heard they were in Arizona selling art at flea markets or some shit like that. I still keep tabs on them, because if the day should ever come that they get back on their feet, I will do everything in my power to destroy them again.

Delia exchanges letters with Carl every once in a while, but I monitor that shit closely. It's my job to protect her heart no matter what she says.

In the beginning she'd been worried about offending Vito, but he'd been somewhat more understanding than I. I guess it could be because Carl had been sent away for ten years. Seems the law really frowns upon one of its own crossing the line, even if it was military and not law enforcement.

Now we're having one of our rare mornings alone. The baby is still asleep, the sun has yet to make it's appearance, and our side of the house is quiet.

"We haven't played in a long time little girl." I whispered in her ear, as my fingers were busy warming her up. She was wet and silky smooth inside as I strummed her.

Her little hand reached down and took my hardness as I rubbed my leaking cock head against her inner thigh.
"Get the rope babygirl." I could barely remove my fingers long enough to let her leave the bed.

Licking her sweetness from my fingers, I watched as she went to the chest to remove the binding rope.
"Come up here." Taking her tiny waist in my hands, I brought her over my face so I could first scent, then lick her.

Clutching her round ass cheeks in my hands, I ate her out as she played with her tits. The sight of her high, full breasts always made me want to cum all over her. My dick twitched at the image.

I grew even harder as she rode my tongue.
"Hmmmmm, so good."
"Hold onto the bed." I tongue fucked her while using one hand to beat my meat.

"I want you to ride my cock. I need to fuck you hard, I haven't fucked the shit out of you in way too long." I set her aside so I could tie her arms and legs in place first, taking all control. I can do whatever I want with her body when she's tied up like this. I plan to.

With her hands tied to her ankles behind her, I pulled her down on my jutting cock, pulling on the rope, making her pussy tighter. She rode me up and down as her juices ran down onto my groin, her sweet pussy fitting me like a glove.

"Yeah babygirl ride that cock...sweet pussy." Her body shook as I fucked up into her with my hand wrapped around her throat, choking and releasing so I could feel the answering twitch in her cunt.

Taking one of her nipples in my mouth I bit and pulled until she screamed and her milk burst onto my tongue. "Ssh…take it." I slapped her ass as I pulled her down roughly on my stiff cock, forcing my fullness into her tight pussy, enjoying the hot tightness.

The way her hands and feet were tied together behind her back made her even tighter and added just enough pain for her to be always on the edge.

I bit the choker of ownership around her neck. "Mine, you'll always be mine...say it."
"I'm yours, only yours...oh yes...it's so good, it's too much…can't stop...cumming."
"Give me your mouth." She groaned as I kissed her, her pussy going wild on my cock as she came.

I increased the force of my thrusts as I too neared fulfillment, my cock beating inside her. "I love you Delia Thornton, with all my heart."
"I love you too Chase." She could barley get the words out as her head fell back and she came again with a loud groan.

"Here it comes baby, I'm gonna flood your pussy with my cum." I came in her unprotected pussy, knowing there was a chance I was breeding her sweet ass again.

The thought gave me new strength and I fucked through my orgasm, the burn of sweet pleasure-pain making my body tremble.

"That's round one." I teased as I released her from her bonds. "When I'm through with you your pussy won't close for at least a day." She squeaked and cupped her pussy. Yeah, like that was gonna stop me.

THE END

You may contact the author @

Jordansilver144@gmail.com

amazon.com/author/jordansilver

https://www.facebook.com/MrsJordanSilver

jordansilver144.wordpress.com

If you enjoyed this tale you may also enjoy these ebooks by Jordan Silver

Lyon's Crew (Book 1 in The Lyon series) B00BP6Q8M2

My Best Friend's Daughter (Book 1 in Sex and Marriage series B00CCCRAM0

Mouth (Book 1 in The Spitfire series) B00DQLWDDW

Passion B00E8HL9WY

Forbidden B00EBSRDAW

Also Jasmine Starr

Pet B00EGY9SKO

Training His Pet B00EKKFIFS

Made in United States
North Haven, CT
17 March 2022